### "Here, let me."

He took the keys from her and clicked open the car door, slid one of the pastry boxes into the passenger seat, and straightened back to his full and impressive height.

"Thank you for having coffee with me," he said. "And for introducing me to something sweet I can sink my… teeth into."

Despite her resolution not to let Ahmed rattle her in any way, Elle felt her face heat again. This was getting out of control. "I need to get in my car and go before you get me accused of public indecency."

He chuckled, his voice low and sexy as it rumbled from deep in his chest. "I'm surprised at you, Princess Elle." And this time, there was no twist of cynicism to his mouth when he called her that. "None of that was even close to threatening the public's decency." As he spoke, he moved closer until his big body was crowding her against the car and Elle was breathing in a deep lungful of his intoxicating scent. Faintly smiling, he dipped his head and showed her what a real threat to public decency felt like.

Dear Reader,

Atlanta is one of my favorite cities. It's a place where the music is hot, everyone is beautiful, and you can easily run into a celebrity at the local health-food store. It's the perfect setting for the Clarks, a family with new money and old-fashioned traditions, and larger-than-life men with enough heat for a slow, Southern August night. Ahmed, the first of these Clark men, came to me in a dream. I hope you find him as wonderful as I do.

With love from Atlanta,

*Lindsay*

# ON-AIR *Passion*

## LINDSAY EVANS

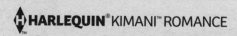

HARLEQUIN® KIMANI™ ROMANCE

Recycling programs
for this product may
not exist in your area.

ISBN-13: 978-1-335-21656-4

On-Air Passion

Copyright © 2018 by Lindsay Evans

For questions and comments about the quality of this book please contact us at CustomerService@Harlequin.com.

**Printed in U.S.A.**

**Lindsay Evans** was born in Jamaica and currently lives and writes in Atlanta, Georgia, where she's constantly on the hunt for inspiration, club in hand. She loves good food and romance and would happily travel to the ends of the earth for both. Find out more at www.lindsayevanswrites.com.

### Books by Lindsay Evans

### Harlequin Kimani Romance

*Pleasure Under the Sun*
*Sultry Pleasure*
*Snowy Mountain Nights*
*Affair of Pleasure*
*Untamed Love*
*Bare Pleasures*
*The Pleasure of His Company*
*On-Air Passion*

Visit the Author Profile page
at Harlequin.com for more titles.

For all my readers, THANK YOU!

# Chapter 1

"You should just keep your mouth shut! Nobody wants to hear politics from a ballplayer."

From behind the broad back of his bodyguard, Ahmed moved quickly through the vocal crowd of about two dozen people to get to the doors of the radio station. Some were obviously gawking simply because of who he was—rich, retired at thirty and a consistent presence in the Atlanta club scene and on gossip sites across the internet. Others were there because they smelled a scandal or something close to it. And there were some who were present, like the guy who'd just screamed at Ahmed, because they apparently didn't have anything better to do at ten o'clock on a Wednesday morning.

"Technically you're an *ex*-ballplayer, so you can

have opinions on anything you damn well please." Sam, Ahmed's bodyguard and cousin, growled the comment as they slid past the radio station's security guys, just low enough for Ahmed to hear, although if he'd said it at the top of his voice, nobody would have reacted. Guys over six feet tall with muscles stacked on top of muscles could get away with saying just about anything they wanted to, and to whomever.

Ahmed was built on a more modest but—he liked to think—no less impressive scale with his six and a half feet of lean but defined muscle, a strong jawline and cheekbones that had been accused a time or two of being "chiseled." And those were just the nice things his sisters said about him.

Only the memory of the mellow breakfast he'd had with his family—his sisters, Aisha and Devyn, his mother and Sam—kept his annoyance at the heckler to a low-grade ripple. Besides, the hostility of strangers was nothing new to him, especially after twelve years playing professional basketball. He was now retired and having fun being a part-time radio show host. Even if he'd been silent about his politics, people would still find some way to throw insults his way. Plenty of his former teammates were prime examples of that. The people loved you when you were playing well, making them money, entertaining them. But once you fumbled, good luck.

"Damn, they're rowdy out there today." Sam settled the lines of his dark jacket more firmly on his shoulders with a shrug, the custom-made suit easily hiding his gun and somehow minimizing the size, but not the threat, of his big body. Ahmed didn't know how he could wear it with the crazy-hot January weather currently punishing Atlanta. "What the hell did you do while I was asleep?" His deep voice rumbled in a way that let Ahmed know he was only half joking. Before going their separate ways—Sam to the military and Ahmed to basketball—Sam was forever pulling Ahmed out of the trouble his big mouth got him into. He'd learned to temper his snarkiness but once Sam got out of the army with an honorable discharge, Sam fell back into the role as bodyguard but in a more official capacity.

"You know it's because of that tweet I sent last night," Ahmed said.

"As if the city didn't already know how you felt about it closing that downtown high school." Sam took in the wide and sterile hallway and the half dozen or so people making their way through it with a skilled gaze, taking in details Ahmed took for granted.

"Just making sure they didn't miss my opinion," he said with a scornful twist of his lips.

Marcus Garvey High was a school Ahmed had poured a lot of money and time into to support its STEM program that worked to give city kids an equal chance at tech, engineering and science jobs once they graduated. Although Ahmed had been born into a middle-class family and hadn't faced the challenges many of those kids at the high school did, he knew betting on an elusive sports career or going into the armed forces shouldn't be the only options they saw in their future.

Ahmed was sick of urban kids' education being a low priority. Something had to be done about securing their future. He may not be a politician or even a "real activist," by some standards but he was doing what he could while he had the platform.

"Don't forget we're going to that town hall meeting on Monday morning," Ahmed said.

"Good," Sam said, nodding.

As they made their way toward the studio Ahmed would occupy for the next three hours, Sam walked just behind and to the right of Ahmed, keeping an eye out for whatever possible dangers lurked nearby. Not that Ahmed had stumbled into any hazards after being at the station for his new gig for nearly two months now. The weekly midmorning show was still enjoyable. It gave him a chance to interact with fans—and haters—in a personal way he'd never had the chance to try before. And it was something for him to do after retirement that didn't involve groupies, the successful string of restaurant franchises he'd bought or the various "investment people" he'd had to hire once his money began multiplying even faster than he'd planned.

Sam stepped ahead to push open the door of the studio, and Ahmed moved to step through it when a flash of pink caught his eye, something unusual in his established Wednesday-morning routine. He stopped in his tracks and damn near caught his breath at the vision of femininity floating toward him from down the hallway.

High heels, a pink floral dress swirling around

slender legs and hips, a narrow waist he could easily measure with both of his hands. The woman's breasts were small, barely a handful, but like most Black men he socialized with, Ahmed had never been caught up in breast size. Big, small, barely there at all—it didn't matter to him. The rear view was what made him decide whether or not a woman was worth a second look or even a second date.

The Pink Lady sauntered toward him, her hips swaying and high heels loudly kissing the tile floors, making his heart beat faster as she came close. She wore her hair straight and pinned up in some sort of topknot with curly wisps floating around her face.

"Don't swallow your tongue." Sam, still holding the door open, was making a visible effort not to roll his eyes.

Ahmed didn't care. He was already losing himself in a daydream involving thick thighs and a plump backside made for spanking. He had no idea what his Pink Lady was packing in her trunk, but *damn*, he bet it was good. His fingers twitched with the phantom sensation of sinking into her sweet flesh.

Sam pretended to cough into his fist. "Okay, now you're just being a creep."

And he was right. Ahmed couldn't stop himself from just...staring. He didn't want to stop. Above her hips and waist and delicate-looking breasts, the woman's face was *pretty*. Like a daisy in sunlight or a rainbow after a storm, she stunned him with her natural and easy radiance. The image came to him, effortlessly, of tumbling with her into his bed to the music of her laughter and the sweet clasp of her thighs while her thick hair fanned over his pillow.

*Damn.* She made him want to give up his rule about messing around at work.

But he wasn't a kid anymore. He couldn't afford to be that sloppy about who he took to his bed. Not again.

His—no—*the* Pink Lady was still walking toward Ahmed, but he forced himself to look away from her.

"Let's get in there and do this." He clapped his hands once, a loud gunshot of a noise to get his mind right.

"I'm not the one who needs the pep talk about sticking to business, cousin." Despite his casual words, Sam did his usual thorough scan of the studio's large outer office, only relaxing his stance once he was satisfied nothing lurked in the spacious room to harm Ahmed on his watch.

"Ahmed, my man!" The station's general manager, Clive Ramirez, was a ball of energy. Probably from the four-plus espressos he usually had before lunch.

He stepped out from behind the receptionist's desk, where he had been looking over the young woman's shoulder at something on her computer. With a wide grin, he shook Ahmed's hand. Firm and enthusiastic.

"What's going on, Clive?"

"Life, just life." Short yet muscular, with a belly just beginning to grow from middle age and lack of exercise, Clive Ramirez gave the impression of being a perennially happy man. He loved what he did for a living, fairly treated the people who worked for him, and loved drama like a teenage girl. But everyone had to have a hobby.

Clive followed Ahmed and Sam from the outer offices to the sound booth.

"Nothing wrong with that." Ahmed took off his blazer and draped it over one of the six chairs in the room while Sam stood with his back against the wall, his legs spread, hands clasped easily in front of him as he kept an eye on the single door into the room and the glass partition separating the sound booth from the studio, where the sound engineer and his intern handled their responsibilities.

Over the airwaves, Ahmed could hear DJ Don Juan, who was in the sound booth across the hall, about to wrap up his morning show.

"What's on tap for today?" Ahmed asked Clive. "Anything special or do I just do my thing?" His *thing* was usually to play music, rile up the listeners and entertain them with what his mother called his bee-sting humor. Ahmed would almost do this for free. He settled down into the ergonomic chair with a sigh of bone-deep pleasure then swiveled around to keep Clive in his sights.

The station's GM sat in the chair on the opposite side of the oblong table and its six microphones set up in the center of the soundproof room. "More of the usual," Clive said. "Except we have a Valentine's Day promotion going on. A local woman is supposed to come on with you today to plug her business." He passed Ahmed a sheet of paper. "It's all here. Just introduce her and her business then offer the prize. If it goes well, people will be calling in to win, and she'll get her money's worth in new clients."

"Cool, I can do that." He quickly scanned the paper, noting the type of business, the name of the owner and what she offered. He smirked before he could get his face under control. "Selling romance, huh?"

"What? You got something against selling love? 'tis the season, my friend."

Ahmed shrugged, not bothering to offer his opinion about romance or love in general. None of the so-called relationships he'd experienced had anything remotely like "love" attached to them. He didn't want to seem like the Grinch or whatever the Valentine's Day equivalent was.

"If you like it, I love it," he said and caught the flicker of amusement on Sam's otherwise stoic face.

Ahmed hid his hand behind his back and shot his cousin the bird. This time, Sam's amusement came with a huff of quiet laughter.

Minutes later, Ahmed eased into the seat, once DJ Don Juan wrapped up his program. He slipped on the headphones and into his on-air persona.

"Hey, Atlanta! It's Ahmed Clark on the air and in your ear for the next—" he looked at his watch, a gift from his father "—two hours and fifty-eight minutes. If you want to talk, call me. If you want to listen, open your ears real wide." And he was off. Grin in place, anticipation for the next few hours bubbling under his skin.

Yeah, he could definitely do this for free.

He fell into the magic of being on air, exchanging laughter and information with his listeners until he got the signal from the sound engineer's intern outside the glass. She flashed him five fingers. Almost time for Gabrielle Marshall to get on the microphone to hawk her goods. He gave Kiara the thumbs-up sign and started to wind down his heated discussion with a listener about citizen responsibility in the digital age. When the woman kept insisting regular people didn't need to share everything they recorded on their cell phones, especially when it came to footage that would inflame the public, Ahmed cut her off with Rihanna's "Desperado."

When Kiara gave him the thirty-second warning, he was ready. The door to the sound booth opened. And it turned out he wasn't prepared.

The Pink Lady from the hallway swept in on a cloud of crisp perfume, like she brought the spirit of autumn in with her, and Ahmed couldn't help but inhale a deep breath of it. The pen he'd been making a note with dropped from his numb fingers and rolled across the notebook, across the desk and then to the floor. He heard Sam snickering. A signal for him to get it together. For real.

But damn, she had dimples. They bracketed her quick smile, and she sank gracefully into the chair across from him to easily fit the headphones over her high swirl of neatly pinned hair. Three diamond studs in varying sizes winked from the lobe of one ear.

"Hi, I'm Gabrielle Marshall," she said. "Most people call me Elle."

Her voice was pure sex. And damn if she wasn't even sweeter looking up close. The smiling lips with just a hint of color. Big Bambi eyes and thick hair he could easily sink his hands into. He forced himself to pay attention to the now instead of the hypothetical future where he had her in his bed. He held out his hand for her to shake.

"Ahmed."

She smiled wider, a curve of glistening and lusciously full lips that made him glad he was sitting down. After releasing her soft hand, he reached under the desk to subtly adjust himself.

Although Sam didn't make another sound, Ahmed could feel his amusement from all the way across the room.

Ahmed cleared his throat and glanced at the timer. "I'll introduce you after this song. You already know what to do, right?"

*Why did that sound dirty?*

The Pink Lady—Elle—nodded and settled her little purse on the desk. Her lips curved again. The pulse of heat in Ahmed's slacks made him wince. A woman's smile. Really? That was what was getting him hard these days? He must really need to get laid. He could easily picture her being the next woman sprawled, wet and panting, in his bed.

"Here we go," he croaked.

The song ended and just about saved Ahmed's life. Or maybe just his pride.

He switched on his mic. "All right, Atlanta. Somebody around here told me Valentine's Day is com-

ing up. It was a woman, so it must be true." Across
from him, Elle gave him a faint smile. "For you fel-
las out there who don't know what to do for your la-
dies, we have some suggestions for you. I could tell
you all about it, but I have somebody here who can
do a much better job." He tilted his head at Elle and
lifted an eyebrow. *Ready?* She nodded. "So instead
of killing cupid before he has a chance to show up,
here's Elle from Romance Perfected to tell you what
you can do for your sweetheart on the day she's expecting more than the usual."

Across from him, Elle adjusted the headphones
and leaned close to the mic. She licked her lips, her
eyes looking with suspicion at the microphone, like
she thought it was going to take a bite out of her. Then
she drew in a silent breath, her features going blank
for a moment. She looked nervous.

Ahmed felt an unexpected surge of protectiveness.
"Tell the listeners what you have for them, Elle."

She flicked a grateful gaze at him before taking
another breath. "Good morning, everyone. I'm Elle
from Romance Perfected. Your local, full-service romance concierge. I'm here to offer you a Valentine's
package of our services—a fully catered day or evening of romance for you and your date." Nervousness
ticked at the corners of her smile, but the warmth in
her voice carried through to the mic.

And *damn*, what a voice it was.

It made Ahmed want to move closer, slide across
the table separating them and put her in his lap for
safekeeping. He imagined horny guys all over At-

lanta wondering what honey-drenched sweetness was pouring down on them through the airwaves. He dragged himself back to the moment to pay attention to what Elle was saying. Concentration, or lack of it, had never been his problem before, no matter how beautiful the woman. Irritation at himself made his tongue sharp.

"You say 'full-service.'" Ahmed made sure the quotes were understood in the tone of his voice. "What are you providing here? Is your dream man or woman included for the night?"

A tiny frown wrinkled Elle's brow. "We don't run an escort service, Mr. Clark." *Ah, the kitten has claws.* "What Romance Perfected provides is a romantic experience tailored to the couple or the person being wooed. We arrange for the flowers, transportation and even the attire for the couple, if necessary. For the date itself, we prepare the perfect location, whether it's a luxury spa, five-star restaurant or rooftop garden."

It actually sounded like dates Ahmed's assistants had arranged for him back when he was playing ball and too lazy to put too much thought into what he wanted to do with the women he took out between games. But Ms. Elle didn't need to know that.

Ahmed leaned toward the mic. "So basically, you create illusions that push poor bastards into believing something like love exists." Now, why the hell did he say that? He opened his mouth to apologize, but she didn't give him the chance.

The confusion cleared from Elle's face, and her

eyes snapped with cool fire. "And you hide behind this microphone to talk trash about people and things you don't know anything about. Love is as real as life gets, and romance is necessary." Elle gripped her purse. "For people like you, I'm sure love doesn't exist. If it did come your way, you'd destroy it just out of spite. Or just cold cynicism."

"The world is cold and cynical, Elle." He leaned hard on her soft name. "Haven't you heard that the bad guys are killing decent folks every day in the streets? Or what people in the world are doing in the name of religion or whatever the excuse of the hour is? You're the one not paying attention to the reality of this world. You can sell love all you want, but the rest of us aren't buying."

Beyond the glass of the sound booth, a flash of movement dragged Ahmed's eyes from Elle. Clive stood behind his assistant frantically dragging his hand across his throat, making the universal gesture for "shut the hell up now." But off the court, Ahmed had never been any good at following directions.

"You should see this woman, y'all," he said into the mic. "She's in the studio looking like some sort of fairy-tale princess in her pink dress with a bunch of flowers on it." He dragged his eyes over her, giving in to the urge to tease her even more, although he'd give away his closet full of classic Jordans to see—and touch—under that seductive dress. Ahmed continued, riled up by the fire in her dark crystal eyes that flamed higher with each word he spoke. "Her shoes are so tall they look dangerous to walk in, and even her name sounds like something unreal and out of a storybook. Elle."

He rolled her name over his tongue, and it felt almost obscene. He hoped the listeners didn't hear it the way he did. Not delicate at all, but rather the low groan of sound he'd love to make while pushing into her soft and welcoming body. Ahmed's stomach muscles clenched with arousal. What the hell was he doing?

Elle wasn't impressed by his words either. Anger glowed in her brown eyes, and the dress shifted over her narrow shoulders and pretty breasts when she straightened in her chair. Ahmed could see the rapid pulse beat in her throat, the quickening breath that made her chest rapidly rise and fall. She looked anything but kittenish now.

"Romance and the celebration of love are an escape from the narrow and dangerous worldview of people like you, Mr. Clark. At Romance Perfected, we're not fooling anyone—we're assuring people of a beautiful experience despite the ugliness the world keeps throwing at us. That doesn't mean I live in a fairy tale, Mr. Clark. It means I'm human, and I have hope. Can you say the same?"

"Hope and delusions are not the same thing, princess," Ahmed said.

And although he was tearing the entire idea of love to shreds, there was nothing more in the world he wanted in that moment than to kiss Elle Marshall's red mouth and the thudding pulse in her neck to show her what the raw side of romance felt like.

# Chapter 2

Ahmed Clark was an ass.

Elle sat stiffly in the chair across from him, her face burning and spine tight, desperately wishing for the whole radio-show ordeal to be over. Sure, he was as gorgeous in person as the pictures her business partner had forced her to look at before she left for the station. But his cocky attitude and rude dismissiveness scrubbed away anything she could have found attractive about him.

They were alone in the room except for the bodyguard standing with his back to the wall, and Elle felt the sudden silence all around her like thunder. She swallowed the thick humiliation in her throat, fighting the heat blasting through her cheeks and all over her face in vain.

"All right, Atlanta. For a chance to win what the fairy-tale princess is offering this morning, call in and tell me the number of points I scored during my last game. The fifteenth caller with the right answer will get the night or afternoon of their dreams."

Of course his question would be something about him.

Elle gritted her teeth, hating his butter-smooth voice that was stupidly perfect for radio. When her business partner, Shaye, had begged her to be the one to go to the studio to talk about Romance Perfected, Elle had initially refused. Shaye loved basketball, was a passionate activist and also happened to be a huge fan of Ahmed Clark.

"I'd make such a fool of myself over him," she'd said to Elle, her hands doing crazy things in the air— her version of excitement. "Can you imagine it, me being on the radio to promote the business and ending up tonguing down Ahmed Clark before he even got the chance to ask me anything professional?"

Unfortunately, Elle could imagine it all very clearly. Shaye was sexually voracious, outspoken and just about always got what she wanted. So, here Elle sat. She clenched her hand around her handbag and fought for patience.

Ahmed had barely finished naming the terms for the contest before the phone lines started lighting up. Somewhere out in the office, an intern or office assistant was answering all the calls that were not number fifteen and giving the caller the disappointing news.

The leather of Ahmed's chair squeaked faintly as

he leaned back, headphones still on, the "on-air" light above the glass partition a bright red that matched the heat in Elle's face.

"Do you know the answer to the question, princess?" he asked into the mic.

She gave him her most contemptuous look. "I have better things to do than worry about the balls you play with."

Laughter burst from Ahmed's throat, and Elle hated how charming it actually sounded. "Now, *that's* something I've never heard before, Atlanta," he said. "Do you believe a word of what this delicate princess says?"

The pet name grated on Elle's nerves with all the power of the insult it no doubt was intended to be. But she wouldn't give him the satisfaction of reacting to it. Elle clasped her hands in her lap and sat back in her own chair, waiting for the moment when she could leave.

They hadn't taken a commercial break to allow the calls to build up. In fact, it was hard to miss the station manager making the "keep going" gesture. He'd apparently changed his mind about cutting Ahmed off. The phones were blinking nonstop. Were both these men for real?

Before they'd gotten on the air, she could have sworn Ahmed Clark actually liked her. In the moments between her walking into the sound booth and starting to talk about the business, he'd looked at her with a familiar spark of attraction in his long-lashed eyes.

But now, he was practically going verbal gladiator on her, intent on hacking her to pieces with the sharp edge of his tongue. This wasn't what she'd come here for, but she'd be damned if she backed out before Romance Perfected could get its money's worth out of the radio spot they had paid for.

The phone in front of Ahmed beeped. He answered with the click of a button.

"Congrats on being the fifteenth caller. Talk to me."

A laughing voice came on the air. "I don't know the answer, but I wanted to say you two should go on a date together. I bet the fireworks would be off the chain."

"Never," Elle said before she could stop herself. She refused to cheapen something that was supposed to be romantic and turn it into a farce.

But outside the glass cage that kept her trapped with Ahmed, the general manager, Clive Ramirez, grinned with an alarming show of teeth, the look on his face clearly saying this was the best idea he'd heard all day.

"Thanks for the suggestion," Ahmed said to the caller. "But I think the princess would prick the air out of all my balls if I even thought of asking her out." Ahmed's grin was infuriating, his tone meant to irritate her.

Elle barely stopped herself from giving him the finger. After all, it was radio not TV. But she had a business to promote. She'd show him a damn princess. She'd be the very picture of poise and graciousness until she got the chance to escape and never see his stupid face in person again.

"Very astute of you," she said past clenched teeth. "And here I thought you were just another pretty face." So much for being gracious.

Clive Ramirez made another motion from his side of the glass. Beside him, his assistant frantically answered call after call.

"All right, thanks for calling with your input. I'll keep it in mind in case I don't plan on having children in the future." He hung up on the caller. "All right, since that number fifteen wasn't it, let's hear some Bruno Mars before we get to that next fifteenth call. Ring me up and tell me something good. I'm ready."

As soon as the song started playing, Elle yanked off her headphones and stood up. She very gently put them on the chair, grabbed her purse and walked out, quietly closing the door behind her. She didn't get two feet before Clive Ramirez was on her, grabbing her hand to shake with an enthusiasm she found more than a little unsettling.

"That was great, Elle!" When had they gotten on a first-name basis? "That spot was awesome. The phones were blazing even before we told listeners to call in. Nice work!"

*Nice work?* It had taken everything inside her not to cuss out Ahmed. Was that all it took to get a pat on the head from another random man these days? Elle pulled her hand back from *Clive* and shifted her feet to conceal her single step back from the man. "Um, thank you. I'm glad you think it went well enough." She made a show of looking at the slender silver watch on her wrist. "I have to get to another meeting. Thank you again for inviting me on the air." *And for humiliating me six ways to Sunday in front of all of Atlanta. Or at least the half that listened to the Ahmed Clark morning show.*

"It was my absolute pleasure. We'll call you with the name of the contest winner so you can make arrangements for them with the prize."

She tried to make it look like she wasn't gritting her teeth. "Great. Looking forward to it."

He tried to shake her hand again, but she shifted her purse to hold it in both hands. "Have a great day," she said with her best fake smile.

Elle waited for Clive's nod, a semblance of politeness remaining despite her immediate desire to walk very quickly away from the station and never return, then she turned on her heel and practically ran out the door.

By the time Elle got back to her office, she was ready to spit nails. Or kill Ahmed Clark with her bare hands. On the drive from the radio station, she'd tried to calm down, but it didn't work. Every time she remembered the things the man had said to her on the air, *for all of Atlanta to hear*, she wanted to scream.

With a clenched jaw, she pushed open the door that led to a row of small ground-floor offices in a plain beige brick building in Kirkwood, not far from her house. The white door rattled as it settled in its frame, and she stood with her back against it, breathing evenly and trying to get her thoughts, anger and embarrassment to settle.

Despite their office building's plain exterior, or maybe because of it, she and her business partner had decided to make their offices anything but. The hardwood floors were gleaming oak, while the walls shimmered from the sumptuous jade green silk wallpaper she and Shaye had picked out together. The wallpaper was as detailed as a painting. On it, a thick and leafless tree spread across all four walls. One branch held a brilliantly colored peacock hovering protectively over his peahen. A graceful and soft peach-colored sofa sat against the back wall of their reception area, and a coffee table with a few artfully scattered magazines waited for idle hands. It was meant to be a very welcoming and subtly sensual space.

Elle inhaled deeply and exhaled, her eyes tracing the plain brushstrokes on the wallpaper that made up the gray of the peahen and the contentment in her eyes while she lay beneath the wing of her beautiful mate. The sight of it, of love as Elle imagined it, usually calmed her. But not today.

"Shaye!"

She shouted her business partner's name and pushed herself off the door, starting toward her own office then nearly colliding with Shaye when she came barreling around the corner. Thick curls spilled over her shoulders and surrounded a face that easily belonged on the cover of a fashion magazine. As usual, Shaye was gorgeous in her club-girl chic. Today's outfit was a flesh-colored and skintight dress that showed off every voluptuous curve. She wore the royal blue Jimmy Choo heels—a lucky thrift-store find—Elle had given her for thirtieth birthday two years before.

"No need to yell," Shaye said with a roll of her eyes. "I heard you from all the way in my office. The sound of your voice could shatter our champagne glasses. Chill, mama. That stuff was expensive."

Shaye was the only one who could talk to Elle like that. Growing up mostly together in the foster care system with no one to care for but each other made the two of them even closer than siblings.

"Better the glasses than that damn man..." Elle made a sound of frustration. "Did you listen to the radio spot?"

Shaye snickered. "As if I'd miss it."

When Elle kept going toward her own office, Shaye fell in step, her longer legs easily keeping up with Elle's furious pace.

"The whole thing was pretty hilarious," Shaye continued. "Even though you were obviously pissed."

"He made me come off like some idiotic child, like I don't know anything about the real world and the crappy things in it."

Elle stepped into her office and dropped into the small love seat under the window while Shaye perched on the corner of her desk, ankles crossed and smiling. Elle wanted to shove her partner off the desk and onto her ass.

"Calm down, sweetie," Shaye said. "Ahmed was just doing that for a laugh and to make the whole advertising give-and-take seem more interesting. He didn't mean anything by it."

"You weren't there. He meant every damn word— "

The sound of her desktop phone ringing cut Elle off. "Who is that?" she asked, too irritated to bother getting up to look herself.

Shaye peeked over at the phone's display. "It looks like the radio station."

"Jesus… What now? They want to humiliate me some more today?" Elle clambered to her feet and answered the phone, putting it on speaker so Shaye could hear, too. She sat down behind the desk. "Romance Perfected. Elle Marshall speaking."

"Elle, long time no chat!" Clive Ramirez's booming voice rang through her office, and Elle exchanged a pained look with Shaye. "I wanted to tell you the latest developments myself."

"What, nobody claimed our prize?"

"Just the opposite, my dear girl! Our phones rang off the hook even after we had a winner. They loved you and Ahmed together."

Elle rolled her eyes. *Those people must love a train wreck, because that's all that was.* "That's good, I suppose. If the business gets some of that love, too." She grabbed a pen and notebook. "So, who won the prize? I'll reach out to them today."

"Well, an interesting thing. The woman who won the prize gave it back to you."

"What?" Elle exchanged another look with Shaye as her stomach sank. *They paid all that money for the radio ad for nothing?* "She doesn't even want to use us for free?" Shaye looked just as horrified as Elle felt.

"No, no. It's not that." Clive's voice rose in a way that did *not* put Elle's mind at ease. "Everyone who called in loves your business idea. This woman included. But she wants you to use the service yourself. For a date with Ahmed."

Elle blinked at the phone, sure she wasn't hearing Clive correctly. "You're joking."

"Nope!" He sounded far too happy with that one word. "I think it's a brilliant idea that has the potential to work out even better for your business and for the station, of course." When Elle didn't say anything, Clive made a low sound of disappointment, obviously tempering his excitement for Elle's benefit. "Listen, I can tell you're reluctant, so why don't I give you the rest of the day to think about it?" Elle glanced at her watch and saw that it was only a few minutes past noon. "Keep in mind how much free publicity this will be for your business," Clive said. "And, to sweeten the deal, I'll even give you back half of the fee you paid for the radio spot."

Shaye started to make frantic motions at Elle from her perch on the corner of Elle's desk. "Tell him you'll do it," she whispered, waving her hands to get Elle's attention, as if Elle could ignore her. "Just say *yes*." Shaye mouthed the words over and over, looking like a fish trying to breathe fresh air.

Elle swiveled in her chair, turning her back to her business partner. "Thank you for the opportunity, Clive. I'll think about it and get back to you."

"I understand. Call me back before five to let me know." He gave her his direct number before hanging up.

"Are you crazy?" Shaye practically shrieked once the call was disconnected. She jumped up from the desk, curls and breasts swaying, hands on her hips. "Call him back right now and tell him you'll do it."

"Are you serious right now?" Elle refused to make herself a target for Ahmed Clark's bitterness and cynicism again. Once was enough.

"Oh, please!" Shaye paced in front of Elle's desk, hands on her hips, high heels sinking into the plush carpeting with each step. "It's just a date. And a date with a rich, hot guy at that. You won't suffer by going out with Ahmed Clark, Elle. Not like how our business is suffering. You *know* we need this."

Shaye was right. And Elle knew it, but…

"Did you hear how he talked to me on freakin' live radio? He dismissed our business like it was some sleazy… I don't know, like a hookup service or something."

"It doesn't matter what he thinks," Shaye said, her voice pleading and soft. She stopped pacing and fixed a plaintive look on Elle. "Once we get Romance Perfected noticed by people who follow and maybe even socialize with Ahmed Clark, the date you went on to make this all possible will be nothing but a distant memory."

"A bad memory," Elle said, already feeling her resolve weakening.

She crossed her arms and dropped back into her

chair, softly cursing. Romance Perfected was a dream she and Shaye had had together for years, a dream that finally materialized in the form of a small business still toddling along on trembling feet. Over a year ago, they'd had to file for Chapter 11. After a lot of hard work, she and Shaye had managed to save their four-year-old business from going under, but they still needed a boost to get fully in the black.

If this small thing was what it took to get Romance Perfected finally where it needed to be, then… Elle spat another string of curses and refused to look up at the triumphant smile she knew Shaye was already wearing.

"Fine," she said with a sigh. "I'll do it."

# *Chapter 3*

"What's got your boxers all twisted this morning?" Sam's question, delivered in his driest tone, followed Ahmed into the back of the town car as he settled into the leather seat in preparation for the ride to the airport.

After a quick glance at his watch to make sure they were going to be on time for the rally, he shrugged at his cousin. "I have no idea what you're talking about."

"Bull."

Sam had a point, though. At the radio station, Ahmed had been too much. He'd mercilessly teased Elle. But it hadn't come off as teasing. Instead, his behavior had come dangerously close to bullying. Good thing Elle could take care of herself. When she'd growled back at him, refusing to back down in the face of all the crap he threw at her, Ahmed had nearly combusted from the heady cocktail of lust and admiration.

The only thing that had saved him from completely losing his mind was a firm mental reminder that this was his job. He was at work, and this was supposed to be all business.

However, that reminder hadn't completely stopped his eyes from gluing themselves to her backside the moment she jumped up from the chair and started to walk away from him.

Satisfied his momently lapse was at an end, he put Elle Marshall firmly out of his mind and himself back on track with the conversation with Sam. "Anyway, it was just entertainment for the folks listening to the show."

"Since when did you give a damn what entertains the people listening to your show?" Sam asked, sprawling on the opposite seat of the town car. "The whole point when you started this gig was to be yourself and give voice to the politics and social issues that matter to you. Not become another kind of mindless clone."

A sound of irritation rumbled from Ahmed's throat. He could never fool Sam, not since they were kids. He didn't even know why he tried. "She got under my skin, and that's all I'm going to say." He leveled a warning glance across the small space. The conversation was over.

But that wasn't the way it worked between them.

Three hours later, Ahmed and Sam stood near the front of a crowd of hundreds in Mississippi, both of them dressed in jeans and T-shirts, while a congressman from Georgia, a nationally respected education advocate, rolled his tremendous voice through the crowd, chiding the state for letting down some of the most vulnerable members of its population.

Ahmed was doing what he could for the kids in Georgia who'd lost their schools and been consistently denied equal educational opportunities. The kids in Mississippi and many underserved parts of the US needed help, too. And he planned on doing what he could to make sure that they got it.

Ahmed shifted and brushed shoulders with a pretty woman crowding him on one side and a taller man, his arm protectively curved around the shoulders of a girl who looked enough like him to be his daughter. The crowd surged with excitement, a mixture of anger and determination, while Congressman Oliver Wilson spoke, his voice loud and moving, from the podium set up in front of City Hall.

Incredibly, reporters had followed Ahmed from the radio station, although it was in an entirely different state. The manic clicks of their cameras, the bursts of flash and their shouted questions grated on his nerves, irritating him more than usual. As always, Ahmed wanted to use his celebrity to draw attention to the things he cared about, but sometimes he wondered if his celebrity status was overshadowing the real work. Still, with the business of making money out of the way, there was nothing else that deserved his energy more than helping his community.

Nearly a thousand people flowed around them, a security nightmare for Sam, but he bore the trials

Ahmed put him through with his nearly superhuman patience.

Ahmed didn't need any security. Not really. Ever since his retirement from professional basketball nearly a year ago, the media's interest in his life had died down. Without the team and the games, and the spotlight that came with it, the groupies had disappeared as had any danger Sam imagined. But Sam had been the only male cousin close to Ahmed's age when they were growing up, so they'd become tight and maintained a brotherly bond. Even when Sam had gone off to fight in Afghanistan in tour after tour, they'd kept in touch through email and occasional Skype calls.

After a close encounter with an IED that left Sam with a Purple Heart and honorable discharge, it only made sense to Ahmed that he invite his cousin to live on his sprawling compound, which already housed Ahmed's mother and two sisters. This time, Sam had come back from overseas even quieter than before, his eyes haunted by things only he could see. Offering and then insisting his cousin take the job as his head of security, and eventually solo bodyguard, gave Ahmed the chance to take care of the cousin who'd been there with him nearly his whole life.

The crowd exploded into applause, its roar of approval at the congressman's words dragging Ahmed back to the present, and he winced. He hadn't been paying attention at all.

Sam nudged him. "Your mind still on that Marshall woman?"

"No, but yours obviously is," Ahmed said. Although it only took a few words to bring "that Marshall woman" squarely back to center stage in his mind.

Ahmed squirmed at how right it felt for her to be there. "She may be sexy, but that doesn't change the fact that she's got stars in her eyes and lives in a world that doesn't exist outside of a storybook." He gestured around them to the other protestors and activists. "*This* is what's important, not setting people up to have unrealistic expectations of each other."

"I doubt she's as naive as you think."

"If you like her so much, why don't *you* ask her out?" Ahmed muttered.

While on the radio hours before, he'd taken the call from the winner of Elle's contest and been blindsided when the woman insisted on giving up the prize of her "perfect date" to him and Elle. Once the surprise wore off, irritation settled in its place, but he'd held his tongue during the phone call, bantering with the woman until the commercial break when he'd politely asked her to reconsider the so-called donation. The woman insisted, saying her husband laughed at the thought of cynical Ahmed Clark on a date with a fairy-tale princess named Elle.

Of course, Clive loved the idea. Ever the publicity hound, he even brought up the idea of filming the date if Elle agreed to it. Ahmed kept his instinctive response—*hell no!*—to himself. He had the feeling Elle would cut that bad idea off at the knees all by herself. She didn't seem the type to punish herself by hanging around somebody she didn't like, not even for publicity, or whatever Clive promised her.

"Right," Sam muttered in response to Ahmed's earlier comment about asking Elle out. "If I went anywhere near that woman, you'd crush my face." Then he snorted, the corners of his eyes crinkling briefly in amusement. "Or at least try to. Hell, Stevie Wonder could see how you were looking at her. You should've just asked her out instead of yanking her pigtails like a damn kid."

Squirming where he stood, Ahmed didn't bother to acknowledge his cousin's truth with a response.

He looked away from Sam and focused deliberately on the reason he was away from Atlanta and his home with his comfortable bed and the kitchen where his mother and sisters were no doubt worrying about his safety. Not that there was anything to be concerned about.

Ahmed settled his hands in his pockets and planted himself more firmly in the moment. He opened his ears and paid attention.

At the end of the rally, nearly three hours later, he was emotionally exhausted and ready to drop. The walk had been longer than any of them had planned. The police showed up but, maybe because of media attention, everyone kept a peaceful presence. Ahmed and Sam made it back to Atlanta in time for a late dinner.

In the kitchen, he stood at the stove sliding an omelet out of the pan and onto a plate when his phone vibrated with a text notification.

"Sam?" He passed his cousin the omelet and pulled his phone from his pocket.

She agreed, the text said. Come into the office before the weekend to talk specifics.

"What's up?" Sam's voice pulled him from his frowning contemplation of the phone. "You look like someone just kicked you in the throat."

An odd feeling swirled in Ahmed's gut. It took him a moment to realize it was disappointment. "Elle Marshall. She just agreed to go on the publicity date."

"Don't pretend that's not something you want to do." Sam poured himself a glass of milk and sat down on the other side of the breakfast bar in the gleaming chrome and black marble kitchen, his voice a rumbling calm that somehow did the opposite of settling Ahmed down. "She's nice enough," Sam said. "The idea of seeing her again doesn't exactly make you sad."

Not sad exactly, but *something*. He moved restlessly around the kitchen, picking up a glass then putting it back to grab something else until what he had in his hands was the clear highball glass he'd started with in the first place. He turned the glass over and over in his hand, grateful that Sam remained quiet—as Sam was apt to do—while his thoughts swirled in too many directions at once.

It wasn't until he was on the verge of putting the glass down again that he pinpointed the feeling. And the cause. Ahmed had been, surprisingly, working his way toward asking Elle out. On the surface of things, it was to apologize for being so aggressive with her on the radio, maybe invite her to lunch or dinner to give himself the chance to prove he wasn't as much of a jerk as she thought. Once the apology had been issued, though, he planned for his intentions to take a more lustful turn.

But not now.

Although he didn't know it and probably wouldn't care if he did actually know, Clive had basically cockedblocked Ahmed.

The thought of Elle going out with him because she wanted more for her business, instead of just wanting him, turned Ahmed all the way off. And made him a little sick. No matter what he'd said about naïveté, maybe he'd had a little bit of that, too. Enough that he'd wanted her and was willing to go against his instincts in order to get her.

"None of that matters now." Ahmed put down the phone. "I'm meeting her and Clive at the station to iron out details."

"Maybe you can ask her out for real then. Before any of this starts."

"Yeah, right." Once a woman saw profit near the end of her goal, anything else was off the table.

He sat across from his cousin with his own omelet and glass of orange juice. "This is all business now," he said. "Besides, you know she wasn't my type anyway."

"Yeah, you mean she's not a random hookup you can take out for some full-contact action and never see again? You're right about that." Sam used his knife and fork on his omelet, his mild gaze meeting Ahmed's.

"Have I told you how much of a pain in the ass you are?" Ahmed asked.

"Not lately." Sam pointed his fork at Ahmed, laughter glinting in his eyes. "You've been slacking."

"I need to fix that," Ahmed said.

But his mind was already wandering back to Elle and the sway of her hips under that pink princess dress. Less than twelve hours after meeting her, the thought of her was like candy coating his tongue. Sweet and lingering.

*Damn*, he thought. *I think I'm in trouble.*

# Chapter 4

Elle didn't want to be anywhere near Ahmed Clark. But that didn't matter since she was stuck with him in the already claustrophobic-feeling general manager's office.

"Relax," Shaye muttered under her breath from her seat next to Elle. "You look like you'd rather be getting a colonoscopy than sitting here with us."

"Sounds accurate," Elle said, shifting to relieve the slight ache in her feet from the lavender stilettos she'd bought weeks before but hadn't had the chance to wear until now.

Getting dressed that morning, she'd reached into her closet for anything that could make her feel outstandingly pretty, needing something to build up her armor against the unsettled feelings Ahmed provoked. The vicious-looking high heels and cool white sheath dress did their job. She crossed her hands over the lavender purse in her lap and waited.

It didn't take long for Ahmed and his ridiculous bodyguard to walk into the office, filling the small space with their bulk and maleness. Elle and Shaye had come early on purpose.

"Good afternoon." Ahmed Clark settled into the leather chair across from the antique-looking wooden desk while his bodyguard took what seemed like his usual place with his back to the wall, his hands loose at his sides.

Clive walked in just behind the two men, smiling wider than Elle thought was humanly possible. Another man, wearing a three-piece suit and carrying an iPhone, trailed behind him and took a seat near Ahmed.

"Good, good! Everybody is here." Clive would've probably clapped his hands if not for the massive coffee cup he carried.

Barely fifteen minutes before, he had welcomed Shaye and Elle into his office, offering them coffee and croissants that Shaye immediately accepted and Elle refused, before doing a disappearing act. Elle was too nervous to eat. Not to mention the last thing she wanted to do was eat in front of Ahmed Clark, get crumbs all over the front of her white dress and give him yet another reason to tease her. Elle straightened her back and showed the men her teeth. Clive sat behind his desk, still grinning.

"This is one of the station's lawyers." He waved

at the suited man who only nodded once at the room
in acknowledgment. "He's here to make sure I don't
agree to anything we can get sued for. Now—" he
set the coffee mug onto the desk with a solid thump
"—I'm glad we could come to an agreement on this."
Then he clapped his hands in a show of barely restrained excitement. "This is going to be a big win
for everybody!"

Elle was sure the actual opposite was true. This
was going to be a disaster. Already, the trepidation
hummed in her belly, twisting it into something like
nausea. Shaye, on the other hand, looked almost as
excited as Clive, her eager gaze flicking between Elle
and Ahmed, dollar signs practically lighting up in
her eyes.

"So, tell me, Clive." Elle deliberately used his first
name like he'd insisted on during that last phone call.
"What do you have in mind?"

"Well, Elle, I'm glad you asked," Clive said.

He flicked his gaze around the room, perhaps to
make sure everybody was paying attention, then he
jumped in, outlining a plan that included Ahmed and
Elle, a night of romance…and cameras.

*Absolutely not.* Elle opened her mouth to disagree.

"No, no cameras, Clive." Ahmed's deep voice rumbled with finality.

He sat with his thighs sprawled in the leather chair,
his pose one of careless comfort, but his eyes were
sharp on Clive with a serious look that made Elle
think of a high-school principal or a daddy with a belt.

Although she wasn't intimidated by Ahmed, she'd never want that particular expression turned on her.

But Clive didn't seem to get it. "But how is the audience gonna know you actually went on the date?" He sounded like a kid being denied his favorite toy.

"They can trust us." Ahmed's voice was firm. "Your guys can take some pictures of us before the date, and Elle can take a couple of selfies during, if she feels like it, but no one is going to follow us around like we're on a damn reality show."

"Well." The lawyer spoke up for the first time. "If you insist on some media documentation, you can have a mini press conference at the beginning of the evening and tell the audience on camera what the plans are for the date. Then you can take a few photos throughout the night, as Mr. Clark recommended."

"Oh, like prom!" Shaye chimed in. Elle almost kicked her.

"Exactly." Clive flashed even more teeth.

The lawyer looked pained.

When he didn't say anything else, Clive went on. "After the date, you come back to the station for a follow-up on-air appearance to talk about the date, how the service went—the goal for this, after all, is to advertise your business, Elle—and how you would change or tailor it to other clients." Clive paused. "A potential AhmElle relationship attached to your business and this station would bring us all to the winner's circle."

"AhmElle?" Elle frowned at Clive.

"You know, like Brangelina or TomKat," he said

with another flash of teeth. "A lot of celebrity couples have names like that."

*Jesus...*

"That's a great idea," Shaye said, her eagerness on full display. She practically wiggled in her chair, attracting the now wide-eyed attention of the lawyer.

Elle's hand twitched with the urge to throw her purse at her best friend, to hell with the delicate lavender leather of the bag. This could all go wrong so easily. For some reason, Ahmed got off on tormenting her, and while she was never one to take any kind of abuse lying down, even when she'd been an orphan growing up in the system, she hated that she had to constantly be on her guard against him. Her skin prickled with uncomfortable heat, and her teeth were on their way to being ground down to a fine powder. He just set her completely on edge.

Damn Shaye for asking her to do this.

Elle tightened her hands on top of her bag. "How long is this farce of a date supposed to last?"

"As long as you two can stand each other, is my recommendation," the lawyer said the same time as Clive offered his own. "We don't have to go as far as filming your walk of shame the next morning." He flashed a smile as he spoke, but Elle didn't get the impression he was joking.

"I told you we don't want anything filmed," she said and thought she caught a look of surprise on Ahmed's face. "Let's just do the bare minimum of what you need to get this thing off the ground."

She prompted Shaye with a look, and her friend

jumped in with her part of the plan, whipping out her iPhone and opening the app with one of her endless lists with the brisk tap of a finger.

"I'll put together one of our best packages for you both—I won't tell you what it is and spoil the surprise, Elle, and that way you can really talk about it on the radio from the perspective of someone being wined and dined and whisked away on a special romantic night."

Across the room, Ahmed shifted his position in the dark leather chair in a way that immediately drew Elle's eyes to the weight between his legs. She quickly looked away, feeling unbalanced.

"We can't do it at night," she said with a pulse of desperation beating in her throat.

"What was that?" Ahmed looked at her, amusement lighting up his dark eyes.

Shaye giggled then moved to Clive's desk, her iPhone screen held out for him to see what else she had planned.

*For God's sake...* "Not like that!" Elle gritted her teeth and fought in vain against the tide of heat rising in her face. "What I mean is I don't want to do anything at night. The date. An afternoon outing should be fine."

Ahmed had the nerve to actually laugh at her, white teeth flashing, the corners of his mouth tucked up. "Why? Do you think you won't be able to resist me if we go out together at night?"

Elle rolled her eyes. "Resisting you won't be a problem," she lied. "But I'd rather not waste any of my weekend nights doing this. I'm sure you feel the same way."

"I doubt you have any idea what I'm feeling, princess." And something unnamed moved across his face, not annoyance exactly but something from the same family.

"I told you not to call me that." The words flew from between her teeth, sharp and cutting, catching even her off guard. Immediately, she regretted her tone.

The hum of conversation in the room between Shaye and Clive stopped. Even the bodyguard's attention flew toward Elle in a snap of his pale brown gaze. But she refused to backtrack.

Ahmed's gaze was as inscrutable as his cousin's. But where his cousin seemed only vaguely curious, Ahmed watched her with a laser-like focus that made her want to squirm in her chair. But she kept absolutely still and met him stare for stare.

He leaned forward in his chair, arms braced against his thighs, a frown between his expressive eyes. "Listen, can we talk privately for a few minutes?"

"No." Elle didn't want to talk with him at all. The thought of being closer to him and in a private space filled her with an anxiety she didn't want to name. "I have nothing to say to you that you can't address right here and now."

If she thought the silence in the room had been disturbing before, it was just about deafening now. Shaye and everyone else in the room stared openly at them. At Elle.

A muscle worked in Ahmed's jaw and he made an audible sound of frustration. "Do you have a problem with me?"

"No, I don't. But you seem to have a problem with *me*." Unease rippled across Elle's shoulders, tightening her muscles painfully. Were any of the potential gains even worth this hassle? "We probably shouldn't do this," she said, fully expecting him to agree with her.

But he shook his head. "We already agreed, so we might as well do this. I don't go back on my word."

"But I do?"

His look loudly said what his mouth did not.

She jumped to her feet. "You don't get to imply—"

But Clive stood up, too. "I think we should all calm down and keep things in perspective." He turned to Elle, but she backed away from him, keeping her arms crossed over her chest and her eyes on Ahmed. "I'm sure Ahmed didn't mean to insult you. He just doesn't get to mingle with polite company very often. Right?" His pointed look in Ahmed's direction only yielded a shrug and setting back of broad shoulders against the leather chair. "Let's do this and get it over with. This promo is a win-win for everybody. We just have to see it through."

"I agree." Shaye tucked away her phone. "Everything will be great. Just smile a little for the camera, look like you don't want to kill each other and we'll all be better off at the end of this thing."

It was like she and Clive had conspired to be the Ahmed and Elle—aka Team Train Wreck—cheerleaders. This wasn't going to work the way either of them planned, Elle could feel it.

Shaye cleared her throat. "I think we're done here. Great decisions, everyone." She took a page from Clive's book and clapped her hands with a sharp note of finality, of a decision made. "I'll put the date together and we'll go from there." Shaye moved closer, lowering her voice. "Are you okay, Elle?" Everything about her body language pleaded with Elle to finish what they'd started with Ahmed and the radio spot.

"Fine." She gave her friend a look that clearly said she wasn't okay. Not by a long shot. Then she pasted a neutral expression on her face. "So, by Friday we'll have this all sorted out?"

"Um…yes." Shaye made a few quick notations in her phone's notes app then went quickly around the room collecting phone numbers from everyone but the bodyguard. "I'll contact Ahmed with the details, and we can arrange the date for this Saturday afternoon?" She made the last bit a question, looking at Elle.

"That sounds good to me. Ahmed?" Elle turned a closed smile on him and waited for him to agree.

"Yes, this Saturday afternoon is fine for me." He glanced briefly around the room, eyes touching each person before landing once more on Elle. "Can Elle and I have the room, please?"

She blinked in surprise. Who the hell did he think he was? She'd already made it clear that she didn't want to talk to him alone. Elle drew herself up to her full height of five foot nine and prepared to refuse his order. But before she could say anything, every-one quickly left the room.

*What the...?*

The door clicked shut behind them all before she could say any of the things ready to fly from her tongue.

"Elle..." Ahmed's tone was almost conciliatory.

But she wasn't in the mood to hear anything he had to say. When he reached out to her, she shrugged off his touch before it could even make contact. Her spine felt tight, brittle enough to snap.

"Everything is fine. We'll do this date then never have to be alone again. As long as we all get our money's worth, right?"

"Wrong." He shoved his hands into the pockets of his slacks and frowned down at her from his much greater height. "Would you just let me apologize?" He barreled on before she could tell him to where to stick his too-late apology. "I know we—" he held up his hands when she opened her mouth to remind him exactly who had started this war "—*I* got off on the wrong foot with you, and I want to say I'm sorry for that. There's no reason we can't go on this so-called date being at least cordial with each other. I don't want to suffer through a couple of hours of your company, and I'm sure you feel the same way about mine."

Just exactly what was his game? Even in the office, he had been flippant to the point of being rude. And now he wanted to kiss and make up? It didn't make any sense. But if he wanted to pretend, she could do it with the best of them.

"Fine," she said. "Apology accepted. All's right with the world. Are you happy now?" But she didn't want for him to answer. She turned on the heel of her lavender stilettos and wrenched open the door. Clive, Shaye and the bodyguard were only a few feet away from the office door. She was surprised the bodyguard had left Ahmed alone with her.

Clive's eyes crinkled with amusement when he saw her. He stepped away from Shaye and approached Elle. "Are you sure we can't have a camera guy follow you and Ahmed that afternoon? He wouldn't be in the way."

Elle barely kept a smile on her face and the civility on her tongue. "No, Clive. Just no."

Shaye appeared at Elle's shoulder while brushing an invisible piece of lint from the clinging material of her blouse. "I think it'll be much more interesting and more fun to have them talk about the date on the air," her friend said, and Clive seemed unable to look away from the nearly caressing motion of her hand on her own chest. "That way, you won't have all that dead air and boring meal chitchat on film. With them back on the radio, you can get to the meat of the story that much faster." Shaye said the word *meat* with far too much pleasure.

But that was apparently what Clive needed to hear. He cleared his throat and lifted his eyes to Shaye's face. "All right. But we'll have a guy get some pics of you two that afternoon. I'll send them over to your place about an hour before you're supposed to leave."

"I'll send you the address," Shaye said.

Elle rolled her eyes. This was turning out to be a bigger farce than she'd ever expected. And it was all Shaye's fault. She cut her eyes at her best friend, but Shaye only smiled placidly back.

It was all right, though. They both knew Shaye owed her big-time for this one.

# Chapter 5

"He's on TV." Shaye popped around the corner from the living room, her cocktail in hand, just as Elle turned off the blender.

"What are you talking about?" She poured her margarita into the extra-large glass with a sugar rim and took a sip. *Yum.* A little too much tequila, but the current situation excused it.

"Ahmed Clark. He's on the news talking about the Garvey High school closing." Shaye dumped a fresh bag of tortilla chips into a bowl and, hugging the bowl to her chest and her drink in one hand, made her way back into the living room. Her plush behind, in cutoff shorts, wiggled away from Elle's sight.

Elle licked a trace of the margarita mixed with sugar crystals from her bottom lip and hummed again with pleasure. Against her will, she thought of Ahmed Clark. The tart and heady flavor of the margarita, potent as hell, was like the effect he had on her senses. Despite his bad manners, despite the not wanting to deal with him one-on-one, she couldn't deny how much faster her heart beat in his presence, how the way he poked and prodded at her like a kid outside a tiger's cage made her feel more energized than she had in years. She frowned. Really? Was his teasing really working on her outside of grade school? Apparently so.

Elle took a healthy sip of her drink, groaning out loud at how good the margarita tasted, how perfect for the hot summer day, and made her slow way to the living room and TV where Ahmed Clark dominated the screen.

She dropped down onto the sofa next to Shaye, who had already started on the chips, dipping them into the bowl of guacamole with one hand while lifting her drink to her lips with the other. Her friend was already Friday-afternoon tipsy.

After the flood of new business that had come in from Elle's appearance on Ahmed's show, she and Shaye decided to take the afternoon off for a little impromptu celebration.

From this side of the screen, it was easier to like Ahmed Clark. His chiseled and handsome face easily belonged on the big screen. The distance and the cameras amplified the energy that crackled around him when he was in any room while making his otherworldly handsomeness almost expected or commonplace. But that wasn't exactly the word she wanted to use. The right words always escaped her where he was concerned.

"It's criminal how he's actually better looking in person. And sexier, too."

Elle rolled her eyes. "He's talking about some serious issues, Shaye. And all you can comment on is his body? You're a mess." As if she hadn't just been thinking about how handsome he looked.

"I can care about educating our youth *and* how juicy that man is. I have no problems multitasking."

After their meeting in Clive's office, Elle had been too furious at her friend to speak to her. It took over twenty-four hours and an invitation to her newly purchased East Point house for Elle to agree to see Shaye. After meeting Elle at the door with the first margarita, Shaye had just kept the drinks coming. So now, at nearly two o'clock in the afternoon, they were both well and truly relaxed, both because of the drinks and because they'd managed to dodge every important topic. Until now, apparently.

"I wish you wouldn't see him as the enemy, though," Shaye said, managing to frown, drink her cocktail and scoop more guacamole toward her mouth at the same time.

"I don't see him as an enemy." On the TV screen, Ahmed Clark walked away from the cameras, his ever-present bodyguard at his side. "I admire what he's doing. I think it's great that he's using his fame for something other than getting more women and more money. A lot of kids look up to him and the other celebrities talking about social justice issues. I think it's amazing what he's doing, getting the discussions about the needs of our community off Facebook and into our living rooms and our kitchens."

Too bad he was such as an ass. She was dreading her so-called date with him.

"Yeah, he's doing some amazing work with the community," Shaye said. "And I like how it's not all talk. He's out there meeting with politicians and donating money, even discussing the creation of a fully funded private school for the neighborhoods affected by this latest round of school closures."

Elle looked at Shaye. "Are you sure you shouldn't have been the one going out on the date with him?" But even as she said it, her stomach clenched in automatic rejection of the idea. Shaye and Ahmed? No way. She didn't look too closely at why.

"I already told you why."

For a second, Elle thought Shaye was reading her mind. Then she remembered what her friend had said a few days before. "Yeah, you said you would just fangirl all over him, but you sound like you would love to go out with him." Again, her stomach cramped and Elle winced.

It really did make sense for the two of them to be together. Ahmed Clark was an activist. He used his fame for good things. Shaye was also an activist. She had a soft heart and was tireless in her work for the community. Although she wore revealing clothes and had a bubbly attitude that might make some people dismiss her, of anyone Elle knew she was the perfect one for a guy like Ahmed Clark.

She was beautiful, knew how to stun with fashion, loved to party and, from all the stories she loved to tell, she loved sex. And all the things that Elle had read about Ahmed in the tabloids pointed to the fact that he loved sex, too. He certainly loved partying. And if all the stories and pictures were telling a little bit of the truth, he loved the groupies, too.

Shaye was better than any groupie. Prettier and loyal. Ahmed Clark could do worse than be with her best friend.

"Don't try to pretend you wouldn't want to beat me up if I ever looked twice in that man's direction." Shaye grinned around a mouthful of her margarita. "Open your lying mouth and tell me that you wouldn't."

"I wouldn't!"

"Liar!"

Shaye fell back into the couch, laughing, and somehow miraculously managed not to spill her drink. After a long time, long enough that it was obvious she was a little tipsy, her face became serious.

"I know you like him, Elle. And it's okay, even if you're not ready to admit it to yourself yet. I would never do that to you."

They didn't have any kind of girl code. Everyone who knew the two of them knew Shaye was the one who had fun and had men while Elle was the one who stayed home and worked hard and sometimes dated but mostly kept to herself.

Elle blushed, thinking of how desperate she must seem to Shaye, then got over herself. They were more than just friends; they were sisters against the world. Nothing was too intimate, and nothing was off-limits for them. Even when she was mad at Shaye, she loved the damn woman. All the parts of her were open to Shaye—the desperate, the loyal, the petty, plus the good things, too. And she was slowly coming to realize that it wasn't desperate to lust after a hot guy, even if he was anything but nice. If women only fell for nice guys, 90 percent of the male population would've wandered off to die in the desert by now.

Elle shook her head. "You know that's nothing. Ahmed is nice, but nothing's happening between us."

"If that's what you want to say right now, that's fine. But I want you to know I would never go after him."

Elle bit her lip. "You know that's not what I'm worried about."

"Yeah. I know I messed up. I know I'm being pushy about this radio spot. And I am sorry that things aren't as smooth as they should be. As they could be. But I have a good feeling about this. I really do."

And just like that, Elle had to laugh. This was her best friend's way of apologizing for getting her stuck in the most awkward situation ever. All was forgiven.

She grabbed her now-empty margarita glass and stood up. "Do you want another one?"

"Hell yeah!"

## Chapter 6

Ahmed wasn't nervous. Not at all.

He stood in his kitchen, not remembering exactly why he was there. His house keys were in his hand, his wallet in his back pocket, the Jag gassed and ready to go. All he had to do was walk out the door. But for some reason, he was stuck in the kitchen trying to remember what it was that he'd forgotten. Butterflies fluttered in his stomach, but he was doing everything in his power to ignore them.

"I've been calling you for nearly an hour now." His sister Devyn burst through the side door, her phone held out in her hand in evidence of all the apparently unanswered calls. Her pretty face, a more delicate version of Ahmed's, with a pointy chin and wide eyes, was scrunched up in annoyance. With her short natural hair, she looked a bit like a pissed-off pixie.

"Are you sure you've been calling the right number?"

Devyn tapped a button on her phone, and a humming buzz from his phone sounded from someplace nearby. It certainly wasn't in his pocket.

"Yep. I was calling the right brother." She disconnected the call and picked up his phone from the middle of the kitchen island, where he must have left it when he was talking with Sam last. "The last five calls were from me," she said drily. "Feel free to ignore them."

He apologized with a shrug—his version of an apology, at least—and tucked the phone into his pocket. "What's up?"

"Are you seriously going to play it that way?"

"What are you talking about now?" Ahmed looked at his watch and briefly stroked its face with his thumb, a nervous gesture he was trying to train himself out of. He had about an hour and a half to get to Elle's place.

"Your date. The thing that everybody in Atlanta knows about except our mother. And she's going to kill you, by the way."

Resigned to the conversation, Ahmed pulled the pitcher of iced tea from the fridge. He was early anyway. By over an hour. It would only take him about twenty minutes to get to Elle's place in Kirkwood. When he brought it to the kitchen island, Devyn already had two glasses waiting.

"Mom is going to be pissed that you're fake dating when you could be seriously finding someone to spend your life with."

"Mom is the only one on the clock," he said.

And it was true. She'd found the love of her life and lost him at the young age of forty-three. She dated occasionally, but she was sure to tell any of the kids, whether or not they asked, that she was just having fun. There was no man in the world for her other than her dead and perfect husband, but there was plenty of play left in her, so she would enjoy the dating experience while it still gave her pleasure. Sometimes Ahmed wished his mother shared a little less with him and his sisters.

She wanted all three of her kids to know what it felt like to have a forever love. Ever since Ahmed turned twenty-five, she'd been trying to get him to take dating seriously, find a woman he could relate to and love the way she had loved her husband.

Ahmed didn't have the heart to tell her he didn't believe in that nonsense. What his parents had found together was an amazing thing. But not everyone was so lucky. Ahmed had found a bloodsucking leech by the name of Christine early on in his ball-playing career, and she had bled him dry of every positive emotion toward love and commitment just as she'd tried to bleed him out of nearly a million dollars. She hadn't gotten the money out of him, but all his belief in love, if it had ever been in him, was gone.

"Mom just wants to see you happy, big head."

He winced at his older sister's annoying name for him, a name she still insisted on calling him even after he'd grown out of his childhood melon head. But it was her way of being close, so he let her have it.

"I'm already happy, Devyn." He poured the iced tea for both of them. "Didn't you see me in *Atlanta Magazine*'s eligible-bachelor list? It says my life is perfect."

"Yeah," she muttered, raising the glass of tea to her mouth. "Good thing I don't believe everything I read. So what's up with this so-called date of yours?"

He leaned into the kitchen island, glad for the grounding coolness of the marble against his forearms. His skin felt overheated in places, cool in others. Was he coming down with something? Did he have to cancel this thing with Elle?

"I thought you knew all about it."

"Don't be a smart-ass. Like everybody else—"

"Except our mother," he interrupted.

"Like everybody except Mama, I heard the show. Imagine my surprise when I tuned in for the Ahmed Clark hour—yeah, yeah, I know it's actually *three* hours—only to hear you flirt school-yard style with a woman who seriously kicked your butt on the radio."

"She didn't kick my butt."

"Yeah, she kinda did." A new voice chimed in over his shoulder.

Ahmed sighed. He moved his arm for his younger sister, who leaned against the breakfast bar with her own glass. She poured herself some iced tea and grinned at Ahmed, an image of bohemian contentment in her flowy dress with her hair in two even plaits tied with pieces of brown leather that dangled down each shoulder. "She totally owned you on air, big brother, and I laughed." To prove it, Aisha laughed again.

"I can't believe Mama didn't hear about this date," Devyn stated.

"Or that she wasn't listening to the show. You know she'd obsessed with everything we do," Aisha said and slapped the countertop with her hand.

"Are we talking about the same Mama? I recall pretty clearly that she's got her own life doing…whatever it is women her age do."

Devyn's mouth twisted. "I see you're not obsessed with what she's doing."

"That's not how it's supposed to work. Mothers give everything to their kids," Ahmed said.

"All we have to do is pay it forward by having more kids and not dying before them," Aisha interjected.

"And this is my cue to get out of here," Ahmed muttered. He tossed back the last swallow of iced tea in his glass and stood up.

"It's not like you to run from a challenge, big head," Devyn teased.

"Yeah, but nosy sisters are a whole other breed." He patted himself down again to make sure he had his wallet and phone. The key to the Jag hung in the utility box in the garage. He'd grab it on his way to get the car.

"Come on, Ahmed. This is just a warm-up for the butt kicking Elle Marshall is gonna give you if you don't get it together."

"No one's getting their butt kicked today." He waggled his eyebrows. "Maybe a butt might get kissed…"

"Ew…inappropriate!" Aisha pretended she was throwing up, complete with gagging noises.

Devyn rolled her eyes. "You wish you'll get that lucky today. From the way you treated her on the radio, you're lucky she doesn't roll you into traffic and spit on you as she drives away."

Jesus. "And now I *really* have to go," Ahmed mumbled. "I thought family was supposed to be on my side."

"I'll be on your side when you're not treating some poor girl like trash just because she dares to like pink hearts."

"Good luck, big brother. You're going to need it." Aisha cackled.

"I'd say I wish you two a good afternoon, but I'd be lying." He put his glass into the sink and took off. "Don't break anything while I'm gone."

He pulled up to Elle's apartment in the taupe-colored Jag to the sight of reporters swarming around like moths latched on to a light. The small building with its modest walls and driveway looked as if it was being treated like the scene of a crime instead of a celebrity puff piece. Ahmed sent a text to let her know he was there then he slowly pulled all the way into the driveway, careful not to run over any of the reporters who stepped ever closer to the tinted windows of the car to get the perfect shot. Why, when he was about to get out of the car anyway?

He shifted the car into Park and turned it off. After taking a deep breath, he got out and headed to her front door. Just as he lifted his hand to ring the bell, the door opened and Elle stepped out. He swallowed in surprised pleasure, taking in the sleek lines of her, not in another princess dress but in princess *pants*, looking like Dorothy Dandridge from one of the movies his mother loved so much. Delicate high heels on her feet, cream-colored cropped pants that hugged her lean body and flattered her behind, a bright yellow blouse that tied at the waist and bared a couple of inches of flat belly. Her straight hair looked pinned and pressed, controlled and superbly feminine at the same time.

Her front door closed behind her and at the slightly panicked look on her face once she saw all the reporters up close, he automatically went to her side, tucked her under his arm.

"What happened to Clive's reporter," he asked, scanning the dozen plus reporters for one who looked like they actually had permission to be there.

Obviously shaken, Elle tucked her face into Ahmed's chest. "He's out there somewhere. Let's just go."

He guided her quickly to the car.

"Oh, my God! Why are there so many of them? Is this how the rest of the date is going to go?"

He hoped not. "It shouldn't. Must be a slow news day. They'll get bored in a minute."

But they didn't get bored. He pulled out of Elle's neighborhood with a tail of nearly half a dozen cars, two of them with reporters hanging out the windows. What the hell? Ahmed hadn't been tailed by this many paps since he'd announced his retirement from basketball.

"I think Clive sold us out." He clenched his teeth.

"Yeah," Elle muttered, staring at the cars in the side window. "Just a little."

One of the cars whipped out from behind them, going at least twenty miles above the speed limit, passed the Jag and took off toward Midtown, where most of the date Shaye had arranged was supposed to happen. He frowned. Did that mean the reporters knew where they were going?

Ahmed pressed the button on the steering wheel for the phone and told it to dial his assistant, Michelle. He put the call on his over-the-ear Bluetooth headset instead of the car's speakers.

"Hey," he said when she answered. "A couple of the reporters look like they're heading in our direction, but they're in front of us. What's going on?"

"I think Clive leaked the location of your date." The sound of nails clicking against a keyboard came through the phone. "Yep. There's some online paparazzi chatter about that French restaurant on the north side. The source is pretty obvious."

Ahmed cursed as Michelle confirmed his suspicions. He knew the publicity game very well and trusted Clive to know it even better. The man was shrewd as hell and hadn't made it to the top of the radio business in Atlanta and most of the southeast by flinching away from cold, hard financial facts. Ahmed's eyes flicked to Elle.

In the passenger seat beside him, she held herself stiffly, staring every now and then at the cars following them, her fingers picking at the leather of her little yellow purse.

*She must have a closet full of those things*, Ahmed thought.

There was something vulnerable and soft about her then, something he hadn't seen before. Even though he'd called her a princess and cursed the lies she told in the name of perpetuating something that didn't exist, she'd never looked in need of rescuing before. Certainly not from Clive's scheme and certainly not from Ahmed. And he had to admit he had acted a damn fool with her since they'd met.

Maybe it was time he stopped acting like a villain and behaved like a prince for her instead. Just this once. Since she seemed to believe in that sort of thing.

"Okay, thanks, Michelle. I'll handle it."

"I never doubted you for a second, Ahmed." Her tone was at its driest. He hung up on her.

Then he took care of it.

After another quick look at the direction the rogue reporters had disappeared to, Ahmed made a split-second decision. He kept his car slow, going just the speed limit as he cruised along Ponce de Leon Avenue until he saw a yellow light. Then he sped up, blasting through the yellow light and turning a sharp corner, wondering briefly if he should back up his plan with a change of car. His phone rang.

"What's up, Sam?"

"The reporters are still following you."

"I know." Despite having had the discussion about the date being escort-free, his cousin had insisted on following them. Though Ahmed didn't see what good it did for Sam to follow in a separate car if someone was determined to end him.

A beat of silence. "Pull up at the Trader Joe's on Monroe. I'll be there in less than three minutes, and we can switch cars."

Ahmed nodded, although his cousin obviously couldn't see him. "Perfect. See you in two."

Elle tilted her head at him, eyes wide with questions. "You don't have to go through all this trouble of avoiding the reporters. It's fine."

"It's more fun this way," he said, flashing her a grin. "Make them work for it."

"There's no need for you to test them."

"You haven't seen me testing them yet," he murmured.

At Trader Joe's, he easily spotted his cousin's wide-shouldered frame and the dark gray Honda he drove.

"You ready for a minor adventure?" he said, already getting out of the car to help Elle with her door.

She shrugged, looking intrigued. The transfer went smoothly enough. Sam left the key in the car and the engine running while Ahmed did the same, and then they were on the road again, the Honda that Sam took care of himself whisking them quickly through Midtown.

"Where to now?" she asked.

"You'll see."

She watched the scenery as they drove, eyes dipping every so often to Ahmed in a way he felt like a faint brush of heat against his skin. Damn. He really needed to get laid if he was reacting to her this way. He shifted gears and sped up.

"This doesn't look familiar," she said when they drew closer to their destination. "Shaye must be trying something new without letting me know. We don't have dates planned out this way."

"Maybe she wants to surprise you."

Elle snorted. "I don't know if I'm in the mood for any more of her surprises. The last one was more than enough."

Since Ahmed had no idea what she was talking about, he only shrugged and kept driving. The Honda slid sleekly through the streets of Midtown Atlanta, heading to a place he wasn't quite sure was the best date idea for a woman like this, but he also knew wasn't the worst. The way she held herself in his car, delicate and vulnerable, made him want to share something precious with her. Something good.

"We're almost there," he said.

It wasn't a decision he'd consciously made, bringing her to this place. Peaceful. Not meant for the type of publicity Clive had in mind. But after the talk of relationships and dates and making his mother happy, Ahmed realized this was perfect. And part of him hoped Elle would enjoy it.

He downshifted and slowed the car on the long

paved road leading into the small town that had been settled by one of the first Black people to own property in that part of Georgia. Others had followed, and they had refused to be chased out by the KKK when they had begun their massive terrorization of Black people. The settlers had stayed, their courage backed by the number of their guns and the sheer stubbornness of these pioneer men and women.

He tapped a button, and the liquid pulse of The Weeknd's latest single drifted into the car. When he said nothing else, Elle slowly relaxed, her spine curving to meet the leather of the passenger seat, the grip on her purse loosening until she was leaning back against the headrest. She kept her gaze outside the window and watched the urban landscape of Atlanta proper fall behind them, tall buildings giving way to the smaller constructions, billboards and trees.

The silence between them felt peaceful.

A long while later, Elle hummed with pleasure. "This is pretty."

The tone of her voice clearly said she was surprised he even knew a place like this existed.

"Maybe I'll just leave you here so you'll blend in."

"I don't know if that's a threat or a compliment."

Ahmed shrugged. He didn't know either. An unsteadiness reminiscent of his teenage years gripped him, pushing him to get a response whether negative or positive. He tipped his gaze to her again and pulled the car into a parking spot surrounded by a tall ring of blossoming trees. The winter flowers were practically unheard of in most other places in Georgia, but not here. He imagined the purple blooms crushed under the car tires were bursting a sweet smell into the air. He turned off the car, and before he could get to Elle's door and escort her out of the low-slung Honda, she gracefully climbed out. An impressive feat in the bright yellow high heels.

Ahmed closed the car door behind her and locked it with an electronic chirp. "Ready?"

"As ever."

Elle turned to take in the small town, and the subtle flare of Elle's hips and the curve of her butt under cream cotton caught and held Ahmed's attention. She would fit perfectly in his lap. He could practically feel the way she would wriggle on top of him. The crease of her butt pressing down— He cleared his throat and shifted to hide his growing…interest. Trying to look casual about it, he shoved his hands into the pockets of his slacks.

"Welcome to Valerian," he said roughly.

Elle leveled a curious look at him over her shoulder.

To take his mind off his not-so-little problem, he tried to imagine the small town through her eyes. Rural Georgia, a little place nearly an hour from Atlanta and firmly trapped decades in the past. The town was primarily Black now and had been for decades, with thriving businesses on the tree-lined streets, a light breeze moving through the glistening leaves and an old Baptist church on the corner, red brick and beautiful, with stained glass windows. From nearby, he could hear the music. Something old-fashioned and timeless he'd heard his mother singing a time or three.

Ahmed always thought he would move back to Valerian one day. The town was small, a place where everyone knew each other and parented each other's children and looked out for each other. But that was before basketball and fame and everything else that came along with it. He liked Atlanta and everything he had found there, but sometimes he wanted something slower, something different.

And speaking of different...

For a moment Elle gazed around with pleasure, it seemed, enjoying Valerian just as he did, the simple pleasure of it on her face. But when her eyes met his, she straightened her spine as if steeling herself for battle. She tucked that silly purse of hers under her arm and turned her entire body to face him, fake smile firmly in place.

"Where to now?"

Ahmed pocketed his keys and stopped himself from the unexpected impulse to give her his arm.

"Now we go." He gestured in the direction of the music.

At a few minutes past one o'clock on a Saturday, Valerian was at its liveliest. The kids were out of school and had their parents with them, workhorses and worker bees let out for the weekend. The day throbbed with freedom.

"Oh, this is really nice."

Their walk took them from the parking lot—more scenic than some picnic spots Ahmed had seen in other places—and through the small town center, its avenues lined with low trees and the smell of summer flowers in the air.

"I've never been to this part of Georgia before." She blinked down at a ponytailed girl who walked past holding her mother's hand. The girl looked at Elle with wide eyes. "I'm more of a city girl. I don't think I've ever left the city limits for more than gas or to go to the farmers' market."

"There's a whole other world out here," he said.

The little girl was still walking, still staring back at Elle, who hadn't stopped smiling. The child seemed entranced, and the wonder in her eyes only disappeared when she turned the corner, tugged along by what Ahmed assumed was her mother's gentle hand. Kids liked Elle, he couldn't help but notice. Or at least that kid had. He opened his mouth to ask if she wanted children, but that seemed like too much of a "real date" conversation.

"We're heading this way." He gestured in the direction the curious little girl had disappeared.

They turned the corner and walked into Valerian's celebration of summertime in winter.

"Oh!" Elle's eyes widened in delight.

It looked like the entire town had turned out for the annual festival and ice-cream social. Stretched out across the park and flowing like one of Elle's fairy tales through the center of town, the festival to celebrate the birthday of the town's founder was a feast of color. Women with flowers twined in their hair, a stage where a live band played "Treat Her Like a

Lady," stalls selling the arts and crafts of the townspeople and jams and jellies, a Ferris wheel turning
lazily while the music of laughter drifted all around it.

A chorus of happy shrieks from behind him
warned Ahmed just in time to tug Elle toward him
and prevent her from getting trampled by nearly a
dozen giggling girls who were chasing each other.
The girl in front had a clear bag of brightly colored
candy clutched in one fist.

"Wow! I didn't know places like this existed so
close to the city. Or..." Elle looked even more amazed
when the milk-delivery truck passed them with the
driver in starched white behind the wheel of the open-
side van that looked like a white version of a UPS
truck. "Is this a hologram or something? It seems so
perfect. Almost unreal."

She didn't seem to notice that her hands were
pressed against Ahmed's chest, her laughter soft and
breathless as she paid more attention to the people and
the town than to him, the man holding her. But he was
very aware of how close they were. He stroked a light
hand down her back and slowly released her. After a
flickering glance at him, Elle's laughter trailed away
and she stepped back. He could almost see the blush
in her chestnut cheeks.

"It's real enough," he said, thinking of the blissful years he'd spent in the town as a kid before his
family moved south to Atlanta. "I wouldn't trade it
for Atlanta, though."

"Me either," she agreed and began walking again,
her gaze sweeping up to take in the towering mag-

nolia and ginkgo trees. "But I bet the fall season up here is incredible."

Elle strolled on at his side, her little purse held in front of her with both hands, graceful like a fawn, the swing of her slender hips pulling his eyes again and again.

"Yes, incredible," he said, looking away from her hips. He didn't need her as a distraction, this candy confection of a woman to make him see things that weren't there. That there was more to her beauty than just obvious good looks and the normal pull of lust.

He rubbed a thumb over the face of his watch, felt the tiny nick in the glass. "How about an ice-cream cone?"

"Why? Are you trying to bribe me into shutting up?"

"Come on. This is supposed to be a date. Something fun. We should put aside any animosity—"

Elle jumped in and tried to cut him off. "Animosity? There's no animosity here."

But he pushed on. "Let's just have as good enough a time as we can and get this over with. Whether you call it animosity or the strong desire to disagree with me often."

Elle rolled her eyes, still walking in that seductive and slow stroll of hers that turned Ahmed's mind to mush. She wasn't like the other women he'd been into before. Her beautiful but prickly exterior only made him want to get closer to her, to risk the thorns just to sample a hint of that sweetness he'd seen before he'd turned her sour with his hasty words the day they'd met.

"Nobody promised today was going to be fun," Elle said. "If fun was what you wanted, you should have gone to one of your groupies."

Damn, he was tired of people talking about these nonexistent groupies of his. "Can we just leave these imaginary groupies out of this?"

"What? Is one waiting for you at home as we speak—a palate cleanser, so to speak?" Her look was scornful and amused at the same time.

The pavement gave way to grass under their feet, then to the organized chaos of the rows of food stalls. Ice cream and fried Oreos. Funnel cakes and hot dogs. Despite his late breakfast, the mix of smells made Ahmed's stomach growl. Food wasn't the only thing he wanted in his mouth, though.

"You have a very dirty imagination," he said. "Under normal circumstances, I would be more intrigued by it."

Elle snorted. "You're such a child."

Ahmed couldn't resist. "That's not what the groupies say."

She made the same noise and kept walking, her intrigued gaze roaming over each food vendor they passed. "I thought you didn't want to talk about your groupies."

"You brought it up." The sway of her hips was damn near hypnotic. Ahmed's feet stuttered to a halt. He watched Elle for a long while before he realized she was actually walking away from him. When he caught up to her, he brought a vanilla ice-cream cone with him.

She arched an eyebrow. "Only one?"

"It's for you, of course."

Her lips pursed and a hint of wickedness flashed behind the deliberately blank look. "Vanilla isn't quite my style."

*Really?* His mind immediately tumbled into murky waters, images of her tied up and getting spanked by his hand making the rounds before he heard the rest of what she had to say. "—strawberry is more my speed." *Of course.* Pink ice cream.

But he had to laugh at himself, and reevaluate his thoughts about Elle.

Her comments about assorted flavors of ice cream included, she was nothing like he'd expected. In the bright winter sunlight, she was still hypnotically alluring—her voice, the way she walked, even her laugh. But she was also comfortable to talk with, funny, even interesting beyond his sexual attraction to her.

It didn't fit with his initial impression of her, of a woman living in a dream world, selling lies of love and perfect romance when it was painfully obvious those things didn't exist.

"What made you decide to start your business?"

"Why do you ask?"

"Why can't I just be making conversation?"

Elle made a disbelieving noise, a cough of sound from her elegant red mouth. "You make me crazy, you say things to get under my skin, you don't just *make conversation*." She scoffed again, her eyes rolling skyward.

"I don't think I'm that guy," he said.

"Well, you *are* that guy." She smirked and bit the top off her ice cream. A wince told Ahmed she immediately regretted the action.

"Careful or you'll get brain freeze. And you know I *will* laugh at you."

"Well, of course you would." Elle took a cautious lick of her ice cream this time and Ahmed's stomach clenched in a heated, instantaneous reaction.

Her eyes caught whatever transparent expression he wore and she smiled mischievously before leaning the ice cream his way to taste. Since he didn't think she really wanted to share, he took a healthy mouthful and watched her squawk with indignation and pull the cone away from him.

The sweet cream on his tongue tasted like a promise.

"Ahmed Clark!"

Reluctantly, he turned away from Elle's almost-flirtatious smile when he heard a familiar voice call out his name. He swallowed the bit of sweetness in his mouth.

Jonetta Greenlaw, his mother's best friend, floated down the narrow sidewalk toward them in yoga pants and a flowing purple blouse, which fluttered around her knees. From several feet away, she held her arms wide to receive a hug from Ahmed. A smile of genuine gladness lit up her otherwise plain face while wisps of her gray hair blew across her forehead from a casual topknot.

"I haven't seen you around here for a while." The

words rang with humor. In Mrs. Greenlaw's eyes, "a while" was more than a week. Ahmed greeted her with a kiss on the cheek, subtly sniffing in appreciation at the scent of warmed sugar and fresh bread that clung to her.

"You know I can't be around you too long, Mrs. G. My heart can't take it."

She smiled at him, silver hair gleaming in the sun. Mrs. Greenlaw threw not-so-subtle glances at Elle, obviously curious. He reeled Elle close with a hand around her slim waist, and she came after only the slightest hesitation, her body settling warm and perfect against his side. "Elle Marshall, please meet Mrs. Jonetta Greenlaw. She makes the best pies in Valerian. And also happens to be the mayor."

A look of surprise flitted across Elle's features, but she moved without hesitation to squeeze Mrs. G's hand and give her a warm smile. "Your town is wonderful, ma'am. It's a pleasure to meet you."

"Thank you." Mrs. G's interrogating gaze missed nothing, Ahmed was sure. The woman was a human information-seeking missile. The CIA would do well to hire her. When he was a kid, she'd found out all his secrets in less time than he'd taken to tuck them away. "We've never seen Ahmed with a woman around here before. I see why he brought you, though. You're so pretty." Her eyes skimmed Elle's body, lingering on her flat stomach, and Ahmed winced at the question he could sense about to fly out of her mouth.

"Do you have any kids, Elle?"

"No, ma'am."

"Do you want any?" came the quickly fired follow-up question.

"Um…sure. If I find the right man."

Damn. It was a clear opening for Mrs. G, and Ahmed cringed as he waited for the inevitable: *Is Ahmed that man?*

"It's good to wait." Mrs. G touched Elle's arm with a wink at Ahmed that she must have thought was subtle. "Not every man is the right father for your children, although they may be just right when it comes to making them."

Elle laughed and leaned into Mrs. G, surprising the hell out of Ahmed. "You're so right. Although it's hard to tell the difference in the heat of the moment."

Mrs. G chortled. "I like her, Ahmed. You should bring her around more often." Then she patted his arm, leaving him with the impression that she'd be on the phone to his mother before she turned the corner. She was almost as irrationally invested in his future family life as his mother.

"She's nice," Elle said, smiling at Mrs. G's retreating figure.

"You would think so."

Elle laughed and this time there was nothing but pure amusement in it. "How do you even know her anyway?"

Ahmed thought back to his days of wanting nothing more than to leave Valerian and live in a big city, feeling stifled by the confines of the town he'd known his whole life. Mrs. G had not only been the town's mayor for a good number of years. She was always involved in politics—she'd either been running for office, in office or defeating an opponent for the job. She was also his mother's best friend and his sisters' godmother. There hadn't been a time when she wasn't in his life.

"She's my mother's best friend," he said, simply. "They went to high school together here, although sometimes I think they were in the womb together, too." Mrs. G and his mother didn't see each other as much since his mother moved into the house on Ahmed's property, but they were on the phone with each other at all hours of the day. He knew very well the sound of his mother's laugh when she was talking to Mrs. G. Joyful and uninhibited. It made him happy just to hear it.

"Your mother is very lucky," Elle said.

"Yeah, they both are. They're lucky to have each other."

The women were close and had gotten even closer after his mother had been widowed after her long marriage and Mrs. G had been after her very brief marriage to a man who'd disappeared under strange circumstances.

"Yeah, I get it," Elle said. "I like to think Shaye is my friend like that, even when she pisses me off. I'm lucky to have her." Her mouth curved up. "And she's damn lucky to have me."

Ahmed didn't doubt that.

Elle quietly ate her ice cream, and Ahmed watched her with a helpless pleasure. She was unfailingly polite as she greeted everyone who glanced at her in fascination, and the residents of Valerian wore smiles of speculation as they looked between her and Ahmed. They really were shameless. He wouldn't be surprised if his mother got an avalanche of phone calls from her friends in town letting her know that her only son had brought a woman with him to the festival.

Just like Mrs. G had fallen under her spell, Ahmed had a feeling his mother would like her, too. At the unwelcome thought, he shifted with unease.

He rushed to fill the silence between them. "When you finish your ice cream, we can have a real meal." Ahmed pointed Elle toward a BBQ stand with a long line of people already waiting. "You're going to love this."

An hour later, they walked away from Miriam's BBQ rib stand stuffed to bursting. At least Ahmed was. He'd ordered the biggest platter they had, since he hadn't had the ribs in a while and couldn't get anything near as good in the city. Elle at first had played coy, claiming not to be hungry and only nibbling at the straw of her lemonade, but after Ahmed encouraged her to try a bite of the meat that practically dripped from the bone, she ended up eating just about half of the ribs overflowing from the paper plate.

Ahmed tossed the wet wipe into the trash and inspected his fingers for lingering traces of BBQ sauce. Beside him, Elle checked her face and teeth with a mirror from her purse. Although she'd dived into the ribs as enthusiastically as Ahmed, she still managed to look like a cool splash of sorbet in the late-afternoon sun, as if minutes ago she hadn't been fighting with Ahmed for the last piece of meat on their shared plate.

"I could just curl up in a bed and go to sleep right now." She sighed out a contented breath.

Ahmed laughed. If he'd known a serving of good ribs was all it would take to calm this kitten down, he'd have brought her to Miriam's booth as soon as they walked into town. "I don't have a bed for you but how about a bathroom for a quick cleanup?"

She eyed her slender hands with their clear and neatly trimmed nails. "I'll take it."

Ahmed took her to the town's general store, where a freestanding sink with soap and recycled paper towels waited for them in the back. After they washed their hands with soap and hot water, he held the door open for her—the bell jingling merrily above their heads—while she stepped back out into the brilliant sun. Despite the sunshine, a distant rumble of thunder sounded overhead.

Elle pulled a small bottle of lotion from her purse, tucked the purse beneath her arm and smoothed the lotion into her slender hands. The motion was practiced and graceful, and Ahmed watched the delicate movement of her fingers while the aloe-and-lime scent of the lotion suffused the air around them.

"Can I have some of that?"

"Sure." She squirted more lotion into her palm then cursed softly when it splashed everywhere. "Wait." A breathless laugh, eyes flicking up at him in a way that made his throat click. "I just took too much." She tucked her little purse back under her arm and held her hands, streaked white with lotion, out to him. "Here, take some from my hands."

He grasped her hands and hissed quietly at the soft feel of them, the liquid slide of her palm against his that was oddly sensual despite the brisk and business-like motions of her long fingers.

"Thanks." He slid his fingers between hers, getting at the thick smears of white on her silky brown skin.

Elle made a low noise as they touched, warm skin to warm skin.

"Your hands are really soft," Ahmed said, then felt compelled to say more when she frowned up at him. "My mother is a big fan of hydration, inside and out. She hated ashy knees and hands with a passion. That's only one of the things she passed on to her kids."

Elle's tongue darted out to wet the corner of her lips. "That's a...a great lesson to pass on."

"Yeah." Ahmed rubbed his fingers between hers again, a sensuous back-and-forth movement, enjoying the texture and pressure of her slender fingers between his. Then he realized that he was getting carried away rubbing her fingers. And his body reacted accordingly. He drew back. "Thanks for the hydration."

"Anytime." She sounded as breathless as he felt.

*What the hell just happened?*

But he didn't need to dwell on a damn thing. Ahmed shoved his newly moisturized hands into his pockets and dipped his head toward the street. "Shall we?"

"Yes, please." She touched an earlobe where the

trio of tiny diamonds blinked and resettled her purse under her arm.

Ahmed cleared his throat, his mind hunting desperately for a distraction. They passed a historical plaque in front of one of the town's oldest buildings, which now housed a barbershop. He gestured to the sign.

"Valerian was founded by free Black people back in the mid-1700s," he said and paused for Elle to read the green-and-gold sign. Tall and gleaming in the sun, the plaque was as shiny as Ahmed remembered it being during his childhood. "It was one of the few Black towns that wasn't burned out by racist whites over some excuse or other."

Fingers pressed to her lips, Elle made a soft sound of distress. Her eyes moved slowly over the words detailing the founding of the town so many years ago. "Like Rosewood in Florida?"

"Exactly like," he said. "The original Valerian townspeople fought long and hard for their freedom and to keep their way of life here. And, of course, to keep from being lynched." His mouth twisted.

"People are still fighting now for the right to live as they want." Elle crossed her arms over her chest and visibly shivered.

"Yeah, the fight continues all over the world," Ahmed said.

"Although I want to believe differently, something like the Rosewood massacre or the 1921 Tulsa race riot could easily happen again. Even in this age of social media."

Surprise settled like pain in the center of his chest. Not that Elle knew about these things that had happened to Black people in America but that she could imagine it happening again. That didn't fit his image of the fairy-tale princess who believed in ever-after and Prince Charming.

"Human fear and ignorance make it possible for many horrific things to happen," he said quietly.

Elle bit her lip and turned away from the historical plaque. "That's why I'm grateful for people like you... and Shaye." Her lashes fluttered low before she swept them up to meet his gaze. "You get out there and resist the corrupt system and force it to acknowledge what they are doing is wrong. You fight for change, and that's incredible."

"I..." Ahmed didn't know what to say.

He didn't realize she knew about his activism, about how important it was to him, even more important than basketball had been. While he struggled for words, Elle looked over her shoulder at the park, at the couples and groups and children dancing to the music on the grassy slope and the lines of people at the various food carts. Valerian was like a place trapped in some beautiful time in the past, and not the time in the past they always showed on TV, with strange fruit and segregated water fountains and places Black people couldn't find work. It was genuinely a Mayberry-type place. Complete with its own Black sheriff, mayor, newspaper and a history to be proud of.

He gave up his attempt at any meaningless words,

content to simply watch her enjoyment of the place that meant so much to him. As much as Ahmed loved Atlanta—and he loved the city with a passion some men only reserved for the important women in their lives—Valerian would always have a special place in his heart, would always be a sanctuary.

"I'm glad Valerian survived." She turned back to the path before them, sighing, then began walking again. "I wish that every Black town and neighborhood had a story of triumph like this one."

"Me, too."

Their arms brushed as they made their way down the sidewalk in silence. The cobbled sidewalk ended, becoming a stone path flanked by a nearly empty street on one side and acres of green grass on the other. Wildflowers, rushed into bloom by a premature spring, nodded their purple and white heads along the edges of the grassy field. Peaked rooftops appeared above rolling hills. The silhouettes of barns and sprawling houses on the farthest edges of town painted the distant landscape.

Elle's shoes tapped on the stone path, a peaceful tattoo of sound. In that moment, it felt like they were walking on the edge of the world, just the two of them in the quiet, no games, just a man and a woman enjoying each other's company.

"I wonder how Shaye knows this place is here."

At her question, Ahmed's bubble burst.

Any illusions he had about what they were doing abruptly disappeared. This wasn't a real date. If it wasn't for Clive and his machinations, they wouldn't even be here. Not together. Certainly not in Valerian.

With difficulty, he swallowed, annoyed he'd allowed himself to forget that this was all for publicity, that it was not real and that Elle didn't want to be here at all. He shook himself.

*Time to head back to town.*

Ahmed opened his mouth to suggest just that when it started to rain. Delicate and sparkling drops falling from the sky like a sprinkling of diamonds, but rain nonetheless.

Elle looked up with a soft gasp. "My hair!" Her hands flew up to touch the straight wisps of hair already escaping from their elegant twist in the humidity.

Ahmed glanced behind them. Most of the town, with its sheltering buildings and trees, was far back, too far for him and Elle to run without getting soaked. They'd walked farther than he thought.

"I didn't bring an umbrella." He cursed, checking his pockets as if they would miraculously produce one.

A few scattered trees, their branches thick and wide, listed nearby in the rising wind, but he didn't want to chance running under one of them in case of lightning. The date, even if it was a fake one, would definitely be an automatic failure if he got Elle electrocuted before dropping her off at her front door.

Not too far up ahead, the wide shape of a barn beckoned like an oasis. It was a place Ahmed was familiar with from his many visits as a child. The rain was still light enough that they could make it to the barn before being completely drenched.

"Come on," he said.

Elle looked more annoyed than horrified at the rain, holding the little purse above her head in a vain attempt to protect her hair. She squeaked in relief when he pointed to the barn, nose twitching like a put-upon kitten's. After another quick glance skyward, she slipped off her shoes then ran ahead with nothing of the delicate flower at all about her as she pelted toward the barn at a full sprint. Ahmed wasted valuable moments staring after her and the flashing pale soles of her feet, the raindrops catching the light like jewels and falling around Elle, making her flight from him almost beautiful.

Despite her sprint, Ahmed caught up to her easily. Even a woman on a mission to save her hair was no match for a man who'd aggressively and successfully played professional basketball for years. Just past the entrance to the barn, she stopped, breathless and smiling out at the rain, while Ahmed tried not to make it too obvious how much he was staring at her. At her long legs, now that he knew they weren't just for show. Her breasts heaving gently under the suncolored blouse. He shook it off. Whatever *it* was that kept pulling his attention back to Elle.

"That was—" Elle stopped, dropped her shoes near the door and patted her still-lovely hair back into place. "I haven't run in the rain in a long time." Her smile was brilliant enough to replace the sun.

Ahmed ached at how beautiful she was.

The rain came down harder, a rush of sound pattering on the ground outside and the roof above. Despite the thundering sound of the quickly multiplying raindrops, it was a light late-winter sprinkle. Ahmed doubted it would last ten minutes.

Elle moved away from the entranceway of the barn to walk deeper into the smell of hay, previously sun-warmed and now competing with the smell of the winter rain battering the wildflowers and grass outside.

"This is an honest-to-goodness barn." She tucked her purse under her arm and spun in a full circle. "You are just full of surprises today."

"You've never been in a barn before?"

"You know I haven't." Elle pointed to herself. "City girl, remember?"

But, unlike Ahmed would've expected from a so-called city girl out of her depth, she didn't seem like she was searching for an escape. She actually looked intrigued with her new surroundings. With her worry about her hair apparently gone, Elle took in bales of hay and straw-strewed floor with curiosity, peeking into each empty stall that used to house the horses the Troyans—the town's founding family—kept for the children to ride. The mayor had decided keeping the horses so close to the town square was too much of a hazard. Now the horses lived at the Troyan ranch, a modest name for the massive mansion the family occupied on the far western side of town. The barn, though still used to store hay and host the annual pumpkin-carving contest and Halloween party, was largely for show.

Elle stopped near the foot of a tall ladder that disappeared up into a large square opening in the ceiling.

"The hayloft."

But Ahmed had barely gotten the word out before she kicked off her shoes and started to climb, her hands gripping the sides of the ancient ladder, her bare feet moving quickly up each rung. Ahmed looked up and got a nice eyeful of her butt in the snug cream-colored pants.

"What if they keep snakes up there?" he asked, shamelessly speculating about how it would feel to tug those pants down her thighs and palm her narrow hips, cup her rear end and guide her movements in his lap. "Would you be that eager to climb that ladder?"

"Probably." Nearly her entire body was already up in the hayloft, and one remaining foot quickly disappeared from the ladder and past where Ahmed could see. From the hayloft, her voice was muffled but amplified at the same time.

Ahmed shook his head. He followed after her quickly, but by the time he got to the hayloft, the rain had stopped. Crouched in the prickly hay, Elle was looking up at the long, slanted window someone had forgotten to close. The hay beneath the window was only a little damp.

"Oh."

Sunlight poured down through it as if the rain had never been. The wide space was awash with light, the smell of the hay fresh and heady, the entire hayloft an invitation to sit and stay awhile.

"The view from up here is amazing." Elle sank to

the floor and made herself comfortable against a rectangular stack of hay nearly twice her height. Outside the window, all of Valerian lay spread out like a mirage. Church steeples, swaying trees, the houses in a grid formation that made room for miles of green space and the river running through the center of town.

Elle made a soft sound of contentment, an openmouthed sigh. And Ahmed abruptly remembered the flash of the bottoms of her feet and the desire to feel her bare ankles crossed behind his back, to taste her lips and hear her soft voice losing control.

He cleared his throat and made a point of sitting across from her, *not* next to her. The scent of her, kissed with rain and breathless from her sprint, made him want to reach out and touch. Deliberately, he draped his crossed arms over a raised knee. Just in case his body betrayed him again.

"I envy you this," she said after another distracting sigh.

"What?" *My inappropriate arousal?*

"This…history. This town, these people." She paused, nibbling the corner of her lower lip. "Your family."

He frowned. "What about your own history? The town you came from?"

"It's nothing as pretty as this, believe me." She made a dismissive motion and cast another longing glance out the window toward Valerian.

"What, no king and queen of suburbia in your past to give everything their princess wanted?" At the flash of hurt that moved across her face, he could have cut out his own tongue. What was it with him and this princess fixation?

But she quickly erased the look of pain, making it easy for Ahmed to imagine he hadn't seen it. "I definitely didn't have that kind of life," she said. "My parents died in a car accident when I was a kid. I was raised in foster care." She shrugged as if she hadn't just pulled his entire rug of assumptions from under him. "I was too old to adopt, so I aged out at eighteen and started my own life. Me and Shaye. We were lucky to end up with the same foster family in the beginning."

"I'm sorry," Ahmed said, and he was. Now if only he could stop himself from saying these stupid and hurtful things to her.

"What for? You didn't kill my parents." She looked unbothered, but Ahmed had a feeling it was an expression she practiced often, one put on her pretty face to mask whatever discomfort she felt. Or maybe this was another of his assumptions.

"I didn't kill them, true, but I keep saying inappropriate things."

"Why stop now?" Her lips pursed and her eyebrow curved up.

They both started laughing at the same time.

"Damn," Ahmed cursed through his laughter, although he had no idea what was so funny. They were talking about her dead parents for God's sake. "I really am sorry. I'm sorry about your family, and I'm sorry I said the crap I just did. I'm not normally like this."

"So I'm the lucky girl to be the only one to bring this out in you? Charming. It's better than birth control, I guess." She grimaced and turned away, the corners of her mouth still twitching. "Forget I just said that."

"Not gonna happen." If anything, with the mention of birth control his mind was firmly back where it had been minutes before, reveling in the brief fantasy of her panting beneath him, open and wet and begging him not to stop.

"You're such a little prick."

"Not so little, thank you very much." He forced out the comment to get past the dead-parents awkwardness. But even with his attempt at lightening the heaviness he'd dropped between them, something still bothered him.

"So this romance business…"

"What about it? It's doing *great*. Shaye and I couldn't be happier about how Romance Perfected is doing."

"No, no. I don't mean the actual business. I mean your—" he didn't know how to say it without insulting her, so he just went for what he knew "—your insane belief in this stuff you sell. Happily-ever-after, love, all of it. With your parents dead and you being left to fend for yourself in an environment that must have been hellish…" He winced at the rough tone of what he'd said and hoped, unlike before, that she wouldn't be offended. "Shouldn't you believe there's nothing good out in the world? Certainly not happily-ever-afters."

Elle rested her chin on her upraised knees, a thoughtful expression replacing the laughter of before. "Just because I lost my family doesn't mean I don't believe in the *idea* of family. Forming romantic connections is about creating your own bonds even in the face of loss. And if I manage to create my family and it becomes lost to me through death or some other terrible thing, it doesn't make the notion less precious, less happy or beautiful. Bad things happen all the time. The important thing is to be grateful in spite of things that tell us happiness is futile."

It sounded like something Ahmed's mother would say, with one important distinction.

"So you're basically a pessimist. Eat, drink, have sex, for tomorrow we will die?" He deliberately butchered the quote to see the faint smile curve her mouth.

"That's not what I'm saying and you know it." But the light of amusement in her eyes glowed even more. She tipped her head back, and it was the perfect angle for the sun to land on her slender throat and follow the rise of her breasts and the irresistible dip of her waist.

*So damn fine.*

"What did you just say?"

Had he really spoken the thought out loud?

He touched the face of his watch without looking at it. "I was thinking it's fine if you think the world might end tomorrow. Who knows? You could be right."

"Um…okay." But the curve of her mouth deepened. She'd heard exactly what he'd said the first time.

And suddenly Ahmed couldn't think of anything he wanted more than to taste that smile of hers.

He moved before he could second-guess himself, slipping across the few feet of space that separated them to sink down next to her, and she looked at him not in question but expectation, like he wasn't the only one feeling the incredible pull between them. Or maybe he was just looking for an excuse to do what he wanted.

Elle blew out a quick and quiet breath. And Ahmed drew it into his own mouth.

She tasted like sweet cream. Cool and delicious. Addictive. Her tongue licked his, a slow caress that confessed to a wanting he had only hoped for. Elle moaned into their kiss. And his initial impulse to draw out the seduction crumbled entirely to dust.

He pulled her into his chest and she made another soft noise that undid him. Lust flashed through his body like a fever, heating his skin, his blood. Ahmed dragged Elle closer, and she damn near climbed into his lap, licking into his mouth and digging her kitten claws into his chest. God, she was soft…and he was so hard. The hay shifted under them, the scent of it wafting up along with her moans to drive him steadily out of his mind.

He wanted to press her onto her back, to slide between her legs and begin to relieve some of the ache in his lap. Just one kiss and he was already halfway there, pants tight over his arousal, blood pounding, a hand balanced on the ground about to lever her down and follow her with the heat of his body. The slick sound of their kisses seasoned the hayloft.

Ahmed shifted to press his arousal against her. Elle gasped and pulled back, her lips damp from his kisses and faintly bruised. Her gaze dropped to his lap and Ahmed swore her fingers twitched toward him again.

"Elle..." He growled his need, more than ready for her touch.

# *Chapter* 7

Elle was being an idiot. A weak and trembling idiot. But, *God*, it felt good. Desire poured through her, as heady as the first time she'd ever felt it, melting her from the inside out, the arousal from Ahmed's kisses gathering hot and undeniable between her thighs. She felt his runaway heartbeat beneath the press of her fingers, his muscular pecs, a firming nipple beneath her little finger. She flicked the masculine bud with her nail and felt his rumbling growl again.

Her thighs fell open, and Ahmed's fingers slid between them, pressing firmly against her through the cotton of her slacks. She whimpered, a breath from begging him to unzip her. If she didn't stop, they were going to have sex here. In a hayloft. The thought made her moan again. Or that may have been the steady and expert movement of Ahmed's fingers on her clit. Even through the layers of cloth from her slacks and her panties, his touch made her quiver.

He said her name again, a choked-off sound she could well imagine him making during orgasm. But no.

*No.*

Trembling, Elle pulled away from the head-swimming kiss, regret slowly correcting her lapse in judgment. Her mouth tingled like she'd sucked on a deliciously hot pepper, and she immediately wanted more. It would be all too easy to lean into another kiss, open her mouth and her blouse for him, come apart under his sensual kisses and catch aflame in the hidden hayloft. No one else would have to know.

But she would.

She quivered and licked her lips, chasing the remaining taste of him there. Then came completely to her senses. "I…" What the hell could she say after that? She'd only been a heartbeat from begging him to unzip her pants. Elle's cheeks flushed with embarrassment. "That shouldn't have happened."

All the emotion leeched from Ahmed's face and he jerked back, abruptly increasing the space between them while releasing a long and shuddering breath. "You're right." He took another breath. "Sorry about that. I shouldn't have…" He waved vaguely between their bodies.

"It was my fault, too. I—" *wanted to touch you.* But Elle didn't finish the sentence. She'd already allowed things to go too far as it was. She shifted against the hay, aware of it poking through her blouse and into her back and the suddenly sensitive flesh of her butt and thighs. "We should get back."

"Yeah, it's going to be sunset soon," Ahmed said. "I know you don't want to be out with me after dark." If that was supposed to be a joke, it didn't quite make it there.

Embarrassment made Elle's feet clumsy, and she stumbled while trying to stand. She brushed the hay from her slacks and put as much distance as possible between them given the small space. But she could still feel the heat of him against her body, the imprint of his hard chest, his thumping heart.

By annoying contrast, Ahmed rose gracefully to his own feet. "Ready for the next stop?"

She nodded mechanically, desperate to escape the intimacy of the hayloft and the suffocating desire for him to press into her belly and the aching tips of her breasts. "Let's go."

When they got back to his car, Ahmed drove them to The Sweet Shoppe, a candy store in the center of town with locally made toffees, chocolates and confections of all sorts; but Elle had already disconnected from the date and just wanted to go home to her couch and the silence of her house. Still, she tried to be a good sport and kept a smile of sorts on her face while Ahmed showed her around the quaint little shop. She bought Shaye a coconut bar and managed not to make any more of a fool of herself with Ahmed before he pulled the car up to her front door.

The Honda barely came to a stop before she wrenched the door open and scrambled to get out.

"Be careful," Ahmed cautioned. He moved quickly around to her side of the car, probably to help her out, but she was already halfway across the driveway, her house key already in hand.

"I'm fine," Elle muttered, her heels clicking madly across the concrete in her desperation to get away.

"Elle—" he began, but she cut him off to make quick work of the goodbye.

"I'll see you around," she said and unlocked her front door with cold and trembling fingers. "Okay?"

His tall frame made her decently sized front porch feel small and almost claustrophobic, especially with the dissatisfaction that rolled from him in waves. But he didn't push for the conversation he obviously wanted to have. Instead, he bit out a rough sigh. "Okay."

Elle didn't wait for him to walk away. After another brief look at his face, she nodded and quietly closed the door. With her back against the cool wood, she waited through the sound of his fading footsteps on the porch, the chirp of the car's engine as the Honda started up, the ache of emptiness in her chest.

When this day had started, she thought the only thing she'd feel was annoyance at having to put up with Ahmed's unwarranted scorn. But this…this tense arousal, the wish that their date had been real, that things could be simpler between them. These feelings surprised her and not in a good way. The last thing she wanted to be was another groupie whose legs flew open at the mere thought of Ahmed Clark's interest.

"You're back already?" A tousled Shaye came out of the guest bedroom rubbing the sleep out of her eyes. Her long curls tumbled around her shoulders in a messy fall that still managed to be sexy. She wore an oversize T-shirt and yoga pants.

Although she'd mentioned going back to her own place after Elle left with Ahmed, Shaye had apparently changed her mind. It wasn't the first time, and wouldn't be the last, that she made herself at home. Whatever the reason—drunken weekend night or long workday—she was always welcome.

Elle could hear the sound of the television from the guest room and guessed that Shaye had spent the last hour with the TV watching her instead of the other way around. It was only an hour or so past sunset.

"Of course." Elle dropped her purse onto the coffee table and headed for the kitchen, where she grabbed a bottle of sparkling water from the fridge. Shaye followed. "It was an afternoon date, remember? And now it's dark. The date lasted long enough."

"Well, I was hoping you two would hit it off so much you wouldn't even realize what time it was," Shaye said.

Elle turned away to rummage in the cabinet, the excuse of getting a glass the reason to hide her face. "The date went fine. Ahmed Clark is fine."

"Hell yes, he is." Shaye was starting to wake up a little bit more, her voice losing most of its sleepy growl. "If I'd known how things would turn out, I would have happily gone on the radio show to get a date with him. Fake or not, I'd make the most of it." She hovered behind Elle, her presence an interrogating warmth that Elle wasn't yet willing to face. "You did make the most of it, right?"

Her tone made it clear what she thought Elle should have done. Elle hadn't had a date in months and Shaye, who stayed as busy in her personal life as she did in her working life, always urged her to go out more. A woman who sold romance for a living needed to sample her own goods to make sure the stock wasn't stale, Shaye often said. Elle didn't agree.

"He and I got what we both needed out of it," she said.

Shaye sighed with disappointment. "I take it you don't mean mutual orgasms?"

"You take it correctly." Elle turned from pouring the sparkling water in the glass and took a sip. "He's not as bad as I thought, but it's definitely not like that."

But Shaye was watching her carefully. "Did something happen, though?"

"Why do you ask that?"

"Oh, my God! Something did." Shaye's grin was wide and hungry. "Did you make out with him? Did he make you come?"

"Seriously?" Elle stared at her friend, the glass of water hovering near her lips. "How do you go from asking about kisses to someone coming?" But it wasn't that big of a leap. Not really. With a shiver, she remembered the sure curl of Ahmed's fingers against the seam of her slacks, the gentle suction of his mouth around her tongue. Those combined pleasures had brought her close to begging him to do whatever he wanted.

Elle shifted her thighs and quickly drank some of the water to dampen her dry throat. "There was absolutely no direct genital contact."

"That's not what I asked you, but okay." Shaye smirked and brushed past her to pull out a tub of gelato from the fridge. "Want some?"

Elle shook her head. "I'm good."

Normally the sight of the pistachio gelato, one of her favorite flavors, would make Elle grab her own spoon. But she was happy with water for now. Foolish though it was, she wanted to preserve the taste of Ahmed on her lips and the rich flavor of the vanilla ice cream they'd shared in Valerian.

She poured more water in her glass then, after a look over her shoulder to make sure Shaye followed, left the kitchen.

"The date was really good," she said. "I didn't know we had connections outside the city, much less in such a small town like Valerian." She felt a sigh welling up at the memory of how magical the name of the town had sounded on Ahmed's lips. "It's a really cute place. I love the country-sweethearts feel of it."

Shaye came from behind her looking confused and just a little bit crazy with a spoonful of green gelato sticking out of her mouth. "What do you mean 'country sweethearts' feel?" she muttered around the long spoon then, frowning when her words came out garbled, she dragged the spoon from her mouth and licked the ice cream off it before continuing. "I sent you to late lunch at La Bohème Sud after a helicopter ride over Atlanta. I'd *never* send a die-hard city girl like you outside I-285, even for a date with someone as hot as Ahmed Clark." She plopped down beside Elle on the couch.

"Oh…" Elle knew the La Bohème Sud date very well. She was the one who'd arranged the contract with the restaurant and with the helicopter company, too. The restaurant was over-the-top romantic with vintage French decor, decadent food that had been featured on more than one Food Network TV show and also had a fantastic rooftop view of the city. In other words, it was the perfect date place.

Elle had told Shaye more than once that she'd love to go on that exact date with a man interesting enough to enjoy herself with. But the trip to Valerian with Ahmed had been better than that. Unique and romantic. Truly intimate. Even with the friction between her and Ahmed in the beginning.

Shaye wriggled like a maniacal Jessica Rabbit and grinned around the ice cream in her mouth. "He took you someplace else, huh? I mean, our package is damn awesome, but you look like his idea absolutely *killed* it."

Elle rolled her eyes at her friend's enthusiasm. "He… The reporters found out where we were going," she said and told Shaye about their paparazzi chase through Midtown Atlanta, their rescue by Ahmed's bodyguard and the drive up to Valerian. "It was a little overwhelming to realize they were basically stalking us."

Through it all, Ahmed had taken care of her. He made sure the reporters couldn't follow them, and he even tried to calm her down. With the horde of reporters on her front step chasing their car down the street, Elle had been two breaths away from a panic attack. Or a screaming fit.

Even with Clive egging them on, it was still a mystery to her why the reporters thought their date was so newsworthy. Not that she'd been looking but since the radio spot, she'd seen enough old photos of Ahmed with women he'd dated before. No flock of paparazzi stalked him, and at least a few of those women had been semi-famous.

Elle held the cool glass of water in her too-warm palms. "Anyway, the date was fine. Everything went well. It's just too bad it wasn't one of our packages." She turned her mind to the more comfortable realm of business. "Maybe we can make some contacts in Valerian and arrange some things for later."

But even as she said the words, something in her rebelled at the thought of sharing something so unexpected and even…pure about her date with Ahmed with other people. Valerian had welcomed her with open arms, just like Mrs. Greenlaw had, and the fire flash of mutual desire she and Ahmed shared while sheltered within the borders of the small town were precious. She mentally tasted the unexpected word. Yes, she thought, *precious*.

She cleared her throat and tugged at the largest

of the three diamonds in her ear. "Never mind about that. Talk to me about the radio ad. Have the phones been ringing off the hook since the show? Did we get any new clients?"

Valentine's Day, typically their busiest day of the year, was coming up fast.

"Well, it's funny you say that." Shaye grinned and put her gelato away, quickly picking up her phone. If there was one thing that made her happy, it was making money. "The radio spot paid for itself in the first hour you were on air with Ahmed, but look at this." With a few taps on the phone's screen, she brought up the Facebook page for Romance Perfected. "We've had literally over a thousand comments since the date was announced, and our online orders and appointment requests are through the roof." Shaye's eyes practically flashed dollar signs. "Take a look at all these prepaid orders…"

Elle settled in for the conversation. She'd rather talk about this than her growing feelings for Ahmed Clark any day.

## Chapter 8

The fake date with Elle had felt all too real.

By the end of it, Ahmed had wanted to do more than kiss her. A lot more. The desire had taken him over, and in those moments in the hayloft, he would've given anything to bury himself inside her.

For now, the crisp early morning air rushed into his lungs with rhythmic precision. His feet thudded against the paved street, keeping time with his heartbeat as he jogged the road circling the compound.

In reality, it was just a road, nameless and long, that led from the end of his driveway through the mile-and-a-half distance to his mother's two-story colonial house then continued another half mile to Aisha's house. A half mile from there sat the ultra-modern gray box Devyn had built for herself the year before. Just about five miles in total round-trip, a distance Ahmed ran nearly every day, although he rarely stopped on the way to talk to his sisters or mother.

Up ahead, the graceful eaves of his mother's house rose against the pale blue of the sky. A slender female figure crouched in the front garden, a hat perched on her head to protect her from the unseasonably hot January sun. His mother. Ahmed waved in her direction but kept running.

"I hope you're not planning on passing without stopping to talk with your mother," Anita Clark called out to him as he came within a few feet of the house.

If he could've gotten away with it, Ahmed would've sprinted all the way back to his house. He had a bad feeling he knew what was on his mother's mind.

Ahmed's footsteps slowed, but he jogged in place instead of stopping. "I didn't want to interrupt your gardening," he said, which was bull. His mother called him on it, shaking her head and tossing aside the weeds she had gathered in her gloved hands.

"Don't forget, I've known you since before you were born, Ahmed."

"That doesn't make a lot of sense, you know."

"It will make sense to you when you have your own kids."

He winced and wanted nothing more than to take off running down the street and not stop until he was inside his own house. But she'd raised him better than that. "You want to come running with me? I don't want to give up my momentum."

She looked him over, the sun catching in her pale

eyes for a moment. Then she took off her hat and drank from her water bottle. "Sure."

She was already wearing running clothes, capri yoga pants and a tank top under an oversize white shirt with Nikes on her slender feet. If he didn't know any better, he'd swear she'd been lying in wait for him.

Although Ahmed's father had been a fit man, exercising all the way up until he died from his heart attack, it was his mother he'd gotten his athleticism from. She'd been on the basketball team in high school, still played tennis with Mrs. G when she made it back to Valerian for her monthly visits and even taught a water aerobics class at the local YMCA just for fun. His mother stripped off her gloves and the oversize white shirt, draped them both over the porch railing.

"Come on," she said.

He started slowly so she could warm up. It didn't take long before they were running at an even and fast pace, his mother effortlessly keeping up with him despite his longer legs.

They ran for a few minutes in silence, a quiet that Ahmed knew would not last.

"So, are the girls right, did you have a date the other day?"

Ahmed blew out a harsh sigh. Yeah, he should have just worked out on the treadmill like he'd initially planned. But Sam was having one of his bad days and Ahmed gave him his space—for now. He planned on using the excuse of his run through the compound to stop by his cousin's small house behind the pool to check on him.

"It wasn't a date, not really," he said, his breath puffing evenly.

"Did you have a good time?" He bit the inside of his cheek and nearly blushed when his mother laughed. "I guess that's a yes then."

*God.* What was it about this woman that turned him into a stumbling kid again? Oh, right. She was his *mother.*

"So, if you had a good time," his mother continued, getting even deeper into his personal business, "what made it not a date?"

Ahmed wondered how much his sisters had told her. For a long stretch of minutes, he bought some time with the steady pounding of his sneakered feet on the pavement, the puff of his breathing in the morning air. But his mother easily waited him out in silence. Finally, he mentally sighed and bit the bullet.

"Did you hear about the radio show?" he asked her.

"Yes, but I didn't bother looking at the YouTube clip the girls sent me. I figured I'd just ask you first. Save myself the trouble of speculating."

He huffed a soft breath and debated how much to tell her. If there was even anything to reveal. He and Elle were adults. The sparks he'd felt that first morning at the station were mutual. He was both heart-achingly relieved about that and scared out of his mind.

He told his mother everything.

"So," she said when he was done, her breaths even

despite their quick pace. "You have no intention of asking this girl out on a real date?"

"That was never the agreement," he said. Not to mention he was a little worried that, despite the kiss they'd shared, Elle wouldn't be interested in seeing him again. Yes, they'd laid whatever animosity he'd created between them aside. But he'd damn near jumped on her in the hayloft once he realized the attraction was mutual. Wild animals had more self-control than he'd had in that situation. If she hadn't stopped things, he was very sure they would've ended up naked, with hay in uncomfortable places and something scandalous to *not* tell Clive when they met up next to talk about Elle's business.

Maybe that was why she'd clammed up on him and practically threw herself out of the moving car after their date was over.

"Unless you signed some sort of contract, agreements of attraction are made to be broken," his mother said with a breathless laugh. Her face glowed with sweat.

"It's not that easy," Ahmed argued. He realized he was running faster and faster in a subconscious race against the topic of conversation, so he slowed himself down.

His parents had had their love practically handed to them on a bed of roses. They met as freshmen while in the same philosophy class at Emory University, both of them the youngest and most spoiled children in their large families. Ahmed easily imagined them arguing into the night—it was much more comfortable for him to imagine them doing that than other things—while discovering they didn't want to live without each other. They got married before the first semester was even finished.

"Things can be easy if you let them, if you don't try to control them," his mother said.

The thudding of their running shoes against the blacktop washed over Ahmed. It was peaceful at nearly eight in the morning, the risen sun bathing his face in warmth, the temperature only a little cool despite it being winter. Yeah, it was peaceful. Except for the whole being forced to rethink the whole philosophy of his love life.

But what love life?

He didn't have one, and that was the whole point his mother made. He had a lust life. He invited women to hotel rooms and the VIP upstairs rooms of clubs to share his body and his company for a night. But that was it. These encounters were all about control. He'd freely admit that to anyone who asked.

After his breakup with Christine, a woman one Atlanta newspaper had accurately described as a greedy groupie, he hadn't allowed another woman to get close enough to hurt him. Either financially or emotionally. Christine had taken a naive boy with too much money in the bank and trust in his heart then twisted him into this—a man who negated everything his mother believed in.

"What is life worth if you can't control it?" he asked his mother, knowing he sounded like the ass Elle had often accused him of being. But he couldn't stop. "Being out of control without your emotions, with the people you let in, is the first step to losing everything, the second step to sadness." He ran harder, not trying to rein himself in anymore, but his mother kept up with him. "Look at you. Even though you loved Dad, you're *alone*." The word felt like it scraped his throat raw. "And I bet after this great love the two of you had, you never thought you'd end up by yourself. You probably thought you'd raise your kids together, retire together, go visit vineyards in California or some other bougie crap." He hurt himself as much as he hurt his mother with each word he spoke.

But Anita Clark was stronger than his misplaced anger.

"I don't regret falling for your father and creating three beautiful children with him, and I certainly don't regret my life now." Her feet slapped the pavement next to his, running even faster to keep up with him. "Would I have preferred for him to live through that heart attack than being by myself now—"

"Instead of being saddled with a disrespectful son?"

But she ignored him and continued, "I would love to have the greatest love of my life still by my side. But that's not what happened. Love doesn't happen independent of life. And sometimes life screws you, but the love your father and I had never failed me, not once. So no, I don't regret it."

Regret twisted like a sharp knife in Ahmed's belly. Of all the things he'd set out to do today, insulting his mother wasn't one of them. Of anyone, she was the reason he'd come this far and had been able to make the money to help his sisters, his mother and himself.

Ahmed slowed to nearly a stop, his breath coming harder than the fast jog warranted. "I'm sorry," he gasped.

"I know you are, love." She briefly squeezed his arm. "And I know you're still hurting after that Christine business. I wish there was some way I could take that pain away."

Ahmed drew deep breaths in and out, trying to steady himself. Truthfully, he wasn't in pain from what Christine had done to him. Hell, that was almost ten years ago now. It was the mistrust that still lingered. The suspicion that inside every good thing life handed to him was a fanged snake waiting to attack.

He and his mother ran on again in silence.

Long minutes later, a bright-colored car eased down the gray road toward them. Ahmed didn't recognize the vehicle.

"Who's that coming here so early?"

His mother glanced at her watch, her breath slowing. "It's probably for me," she said.

The car, an S-class red Mercedes convertible with darkened windows, slowed as it approached. The driver's-side window slid down.

"Am I early?" A youngish man sat behind the wheel wearing sweats and a baggy University of Miami T-shirt. The look didn't at all mesh with the over-a-quarter-million-dollar car. He grinned up at Ahmed's mother and showed off his bright, if slightly crooked, white teeth and a youth that caught Ahmed by surprise. Was his mother cradle robbing?

Ahmed bristled. "Who are you?"

The young man didn't look at all offended by Ahmed's abrupt tone. If anything, his grin widened. He stuck his hand out the window to shake. "Temple Diallo."

Ahmed hesitated to offer his own sweaty hand.

"Don't be rude, darling." His mother patted his shoulder, although it felt more like a slap.

He held up his sweat-slicked hands and shook his head. "No offense. Even I don't want to touch me right now."

"No worries," Temple said with a gracious dip of his head. Despite his obviously young age, he looked supremely confident in the driver's seat of the Mercedes, simply watching Ahmed and his mother and waiting for…something.

Whatever it was, Ahmed didn't have time. He gestured ahead of him to the road. "I need to finish my run."

"Okay, darling." Without waiting for an invitation, his mother climbed into Temple's car and settled into the ruby-colored leather seats, sweaty clothes and all. The boy didn't seem to mind. "See you later?"

"Yeah…" He looked at Temple's license plate and made a mental note to have Sam check it out later. "Nice chat."

"Wasn't it, though?" Her eyes glittered with amusement. "Let's have dinner later on this evening. And just to satisfy that little birdie of curiosity I see fluttering away in your brain, Temple and I have some investment business to discuss."

"All right." He nodded to the much younger man. "See you later." Then he sprinted all the way back home, consciously not thinking about Elle and how she was driving him straight out of his mind.

# Chapter 9

Shaye spent the rest of Saturday night at Elle's place, giving up her usual date night with the lucky bachelor of the week to go over sales projections and create marketing strategies for Romance Perfected. With the bankruptcy finally behind them and the recent influx of clients from the radio spot, things were starting to look up. Next year, if they maneuvered very carefully, the company might even see a profit. Elle and Shaye worked until well past 3:00 a.m.

Early Sunday morning, Shaye woke up to make coffee then set off for a breakfast date in Buckhead with identical twin male models whose bodies she described in loving detail before speeding off in her yellow Mustang.

With her friend gone and her morning free, Elle

slipped back in bed with a luxurious sigh. But after only a few blissful minutes between the cool sheets, she started thinking about her afternoon with Ahmed. Their kiss. The way he tasted. How the date had ended.

*Bad idea.*

And because she knew when to take a hint, even if it was from her own subconscious—idle minds and all that—she left the bed and got into the shower.

Over an hour later, she walked out of the house, purse swinging, with no particular destination in mind. Once she got in her car and started driving, the destination, decided by the lingering taste of Ahmed on her tongue despite her two teeth brushings and a quick breakfast of oatmeal and fruit, became clear: her favorite bakery in Grant Park.

Yes, she could admit it. Ahmed's kisses made her think of dessert. Of melting and sweetness and all kinds of delicious and wicked things that were bad for her. So, The Baked Good it was.

The bell above the door rang as she pushed into the bakery then held the door open for a woman struggling with two large pastry boxes and a kindergartner who didn't look ready to leave the shop. After a breathless "thank you," the woman rushed out, her young daughter clinging tearfully to her skirt.

The Baked Good smelled like heaven. The little pastry and coffee shop was tucked away in an up-and-coming area that was already home to a few clothing boutiques, an ice-cream parlor and a wine bar. The Baked Good had quickly become one of Elle's favorite places after she discovered it on the way to an appointment at the wine bar. The wine bar she eventually added to Romance Perfected's list of date venues while The Baked Good went on their website as a recommended business.

"Elle!" The young woman behind the counter, voluptuous and gorgeous in an African-print dress that flared out around her generous hips, didn't look older than nineteen, but she was all of twenty-two and the brains behind The Baked Good. "I haven't seen you around here in a while."

"I've been trying to be good, Carole."

The baker winked at her as she finished settling a red velvet cake behind the display case. "Why be good when you can just be good to yourself?"

Elle grinned. "It's your bad influence that made me gain these last ten pounds."

"Girl, since I can't tell about those supposed ten pounds, you must have needed them. At least on that skinny body of yours."

"If you keep those compliments coming, you'll never get rid of me."

"That's been my devious plan all along," Carole said, joining in Elle's delighted laughter.

Still smiling, Elle skimmed the display case, already trying to decide which yummy thing would do the least damage to her figure.

The bell above the door sounded again, but she didn't pay any attention to it, her focus already on a red velvet cupcake with a sprinkling of rainbow hearts on top of its creamy crown. She could practically taste the sweetness of the cream cheese frosting on her tongue. Two of the cupcakes stood side by side. Maybe she could have one now and save the other one for later...

"Good morning." The sound of the familiar voice, unexpected and all too close, made her stand up so fast she almost gave herself whiplash.

Ahmed stood near the door of the shop, looking delicious himself surrounded by the shades of pink and chocolate Carole had used to decorate her bakery. Carole responded warmly to his greeting, but his eyes stayed on Elle.

"I thought that was you," he said with a glance up and down Elle's body. "I'd recognize your—" he cleared his throat "—hair anywhere."

Behind the counter, Carole giggled, not even bothering to pretend she wasn't eavesdropping.

He didn't even have the grace to look embarrassed. He flashed Carole a smile and moved closer to Elle. "It's a nice surprise seeing you again so soon."

Elle was painfully aware of Carole and her attentive ears, but she raised her chin and tried to shake off her self-consciousness. "I felt like a needed a little sweetness in my day."

"After yesterday?" He made it sound like he'd left her soured. But after the night of sensuous dreams and the morning spent remembering his kisses, Elle was anything but. She'd reacted badly in the aftermath of their kiss. That wasn't his fault, though.

She bit the inside of her cheek then abruptly decided on honesty. "Actually, yes." The look on his face made her rush to reassure him. "It was a sweet date. I wanted some more of that for the rest of my weekend."

"And now you're getting more than you asked for." He gestured to himself.

She rolled her eyes but didn't suppress her laugh. "So very true." The warmth in her belly only spread when he nodded. "What are you doing here? I didn't figure you for a man who liked sweets."

He raised an eyebrow in her direction. "I'm not, usually, but I've been making an exception lately."

A tiny butterfly wriggled happily in Elle's stomach at his words. *Watch it, girl.*

"Actually, I saw this place listed on your company's website and thought I'd try it out," he said, turning the wriggle in Elle's stomach into a full flutter. He was checking her out in more ways than one. "I'm getting something for my mother and sisters. I've been a bit on the unbearable side lately."

"Oh, imagine that. I'm glad I'm not the only one who gets the gift of your particular moods."

"I'm a nice enough guy. Or at least I can be."

"Then what do you have to apologize for?"

For a moment, he looked uncomfortable and tossed a gaze toward the counter where Carole was obviously listening. Just then, the store's bell chimed and two women walked in, chatting excitedly about an upcoming wedding. They headed for the counter, and Carole stepped forward to help them. Without Carole's obvious attention, Elle relaxed.

"Tell you what," Ahmed said. "I'll give you all

the gory details over coffee and a…" He looked at her empty hands. "…whatever it is you're having."

"I'll take you up on that offer." *Gladly.*

Once Carole had a break in her discussions with the two new customers, she served Elle one of the cupcakes in the case, a croissant for Ahmed and coffees for them both. They sat at one of the tables far enough away from Carole to give themselves some illusion of privacy.

The table was small and the chairs close. Their knees brushed under the delicate white tablecloth while they leaned in over the pastries and coffees in front of them.

"What terrible thing did you say to your mother and sisters?" Elle asked.

Ahmed tasted his coffee, made a surprised sound of appreciation and went back in for a bigger sip. "They got into my business and wanted to know about our date."

"Oh!" That definitely wasn't something Elle expected. As far as anyone else knew, their date had been all about promotion, arranged by the radio station to get more listeners and advertisers. The good time they'd had that afternoon—before their kiss had jump-started Elle's libido and destroyed her peace of mind—had been accidental. Anyone who listened to Ahmed's show knew it was all pretend.

"They know it was just for the radio station, right?" Elle asked, even as a tiny part of her wanted him to insist it hadn't all been pretend.

"That didn't stop them from hoping."

She dipped her head and toyed with the largest diamond in her ear. Disappointment clogged her throat, for a moment making it hard for her to speak. "Hoping what? I don't imagine you have a shortage of women lined up to go on dates with you."

"In their minds, it's not quantity, it's quality." When Elle didn't say anything—she didn't know *what* to say—he went on. "They're convinced you're a better class of date than the rest and wanted to make sure I didn't mess it up."

Even though the women in his family obviously didn't know her, Elle felt warmed by their opinion. She took a sip of her coffee to hide her smile. "Are you in the habit of messing up your own dates?"

"They seem to think so."

"What do *you* think?"

"I think they need cake."

Elle choked on a laugh. "So, what actually happened?"

On the radio, Ahmed was a natural storyteller, reeling in his audience with his compelling voice and his way of bringing a tale to life. He could do better than the little summary he just gave.

"You seriously want to hear this?"

"Of course. Especially since I know it's about me, or at least about our date." It felt strange to say "our date" versus "the farce," as she had been calling it in her mind. But maybe it had been so long since Elle had been on a real date that now she didn't even know the difference. She mentally rolled her eyes at herself.

He leaned his forearms on the table, and Elle

forced herself to look away from the powerful flex of muscles and focus on what was actually coming out of his mouth. "Okay," he said. "This is what happened."

She propped her chin up on an upraised palm and listened.

*Ahmed felt tired, exhilarated and frustrated at the same time. After the kiss he'd shared with Elle, the arousal hummed steadily through him, amplifying his awareness of his body and distracting the hell out of him. He'd wanted to do much more than kiss Elle. Even the reminder that it really hadn't been a real date, not one they'd both agreed to out of the mutual attraction sizzling between them, hadn't quite done its job to cool him off. Even the awkward way they'd left things hadn't softened his desire. He got home frustrated in every sense of the word.*

*And stumbled into his kitchen to the sight of his sisters at the breakfast bar.*

*"How did the date go?"*

*They were drinking his good wine, a Pinotage he'd picked up on a recent trip to South Africa. He scanned the bottle and saw it was just about empty, which wasn't a difficult feat between the two of them.*

*"It went fine." He tried to walk past them, but Devyn jumped up from her seat and grabbed his arm with one hand, the other clutching a half-gone glass of wine.*

*"Well, you're here instead of being in her bed—"*

*"It's only their first date!" Aisha protested.*

"—*so it mustn't have gone that well,*" Devyn finished.

"*I told you, it's for the radio station, it's not real.*"

"*That's not what that cologne you wore out of here said.*"

"*Or those buttons undone on your shirt.*"

He touched the buttons on his shirt then winced to find that his sister was right—they had been undone while he and Elle had been kissing. And when she dug her nails into his chest, pressing close enough that he felt the imprint of her nipples through the layers of cloth between them.

"*Aha! So you did make out with her.*" Aisha laughed like she'd won some sort of victory.

Devyn shook her head, looking like Ahmed had disappointed her personally and on purpose. "*But he didn't seal the deal.*"

"*For the last time, it wasn't that kind of deal,*" he insisted.

"*I don't believe it.*"

"*It doesn't really matter what you believe.*" His eye caught the nearly empty bottle again, a red he'd been saving for something special. Exactly what, he couldn't say. "*Don't you have wine at your own place to drink?*" he snapped.

"*Are you pissed at us?*" Aisha, his more considerate sister, asked.

Before he could answer, the annoying sister chimed in. "*He just needs to get laid. Probably by this woman he went out with. Look, he practically stinks of sexual frustration.*"

*"Jesus..." He left the kitchen before he could say anything else.*

*At the best of times, he loved having his family close. A shared property and different houses at least a quarter mile apart meant he had the best of both worlds. His sisters weren't normally intrusive. But they also knew he didn't date very often. The women he ended up going out with these days knew the score. Nothing would come of the night or afternoon except decent sex, dinner and hopefully a good time for both parties involved. These women were casual, no one his family would ever meet. But Sam had mentioned Elle. Then Aisha listened to the radio show. And his mother wanted him to be happy, get married and have a family of his own.*

*Ahmed slammed his way out of the kitchen, down the long hallway and up the stairs to his top-floor loft, which served as his bedroom suite. The guilt set in almost immediately.*

He loved his sisters. He loved his family. Elle bit the corner of her mouth and smiled, even though she knew there was a bit of sadness in it. His love for them made her ache for something she'd never had. Worry and intrusive curiosity that stemmed from a sure and selfless love.

"That doesn't sound so bad," she said.

Ahmed shrugged. "It was bad enough. As nosy as they are, they love me. And they're curious about you."

"Did you let them know there's nothing to be curious about? If anything happens between us, I'll probably end up as one of your casual chicks, nothing serious. You should let them know that." But the thought of being one of those emotionless screws twisted unease in Elle's belly.

"That wouldn't happen," he said softly. And something in her chest caught.

Cheeks warming, Elle picked up the cupcake and nibbled on its edge, avoiding the curl of frosting sitting right on top. But her teeth caught a candy, and the sweetness burst across her tongue with an unexpected flavor that made her moan. *Lemon. Huh.* A bit of tart with the sweet.

Ahmed's eyes latched on to her mouth. "Good?"

"Amazing." Elle swiped her finger through the frosting and put it to her mouth. "*Carole is a genius.* She did something different with this one."

The combination of sweet and tart on her tongue was divine, so Elle tasted it again and again, drawing out the pleasure so it would last as long as possible. All the while, she was aware of the way Ahmed watched her, like she was a cupcake he wanted to devour.

"So, you come to this place often?" he eventually asked.

She sucked a smear of frosting from her fingertip. "Did you mean to make that sound like a pickup line? Because..." She gave him a teasing look.

"Are you going to answer the question or not?"

She laughed, the simple pleasure of their conversation, his company, fizzing through her like champagne. His eyes sparkled back at her, and the moment felt…warm, like they were caught in a feedback loop of simple happiness, and it made her laughter bubble up again. "I'm here often enough. I only recommend the places I actually like on my website. And I love this place."

The voices of Carole and the women talking about wedding cakes and the clink of saucers from the couple that had come in and were sitting down to cups of hot chocolate nearby buzzed pleasantly in the background.

"I can see why. I'm not really a dessert kind of guy," Ahmed said. "But the coffee is good."

"Really? You should try her cupcakes. The red velvet ones are my favorite." She stuck an icing-flecked thumb into her mouth. *Hmm. So good.*

He shook his head, but she felt his gaze on her mouth like a physical touch. "None for me, but I'll get a dozen for my sisters and mother to share."

"Don't say you don't like it until you try it." She decided to be generous. "Here, taste."

His eyes flashed dangerously at her. The hunger in them made her stomach clench and sped up her already accelerated pulse.

"Are you sure that's what you want me to do? To taste?" He was asking about more than the damn red velvet cupcake, that much was obvious.

And Elle nearly drowned in the loud and insistent throb of her heart and the pulse beating powerfully between her legs. She licked her lips. Under the table, she shifted her thighs, and the brush of skin on skin made her shiver. "That's not fair," she said in a voice that rasped low.

"Does that mean you changed your mind about giving me a taste?" Ahmed leaned closer, the scent from his body, crisp and intoxicating, rising up to pull her damn near across the table. Beyond words, Elle shook her head.

"Okay," he growled. "Give it to me."

Feeling herself practically moving in slow motion, she tugged the paper from the base of the cupcake, the thin white wrapping releasing with a low and moist noise, and she bit her lip, extending the bottom of the cupcake, free of icing, toward his mouth. She licked her own lips when he opened his mouth, white teeth flashing against his sumptuous skin. He bit into the cupcake. His mouth sealed around the bite, and he held himself there, mouth on her cupcake, eyes plunging into hers. Then slowly, slowly, he drew back and began to chew.

A few moist crumbs clung to his lips, and she fought an irrational jealousy of them. She reached across the table, brushed them from his skin with her thumb and, when the crumbs stuck to her finger, drew it into her mouth.

Ahmed rumbled deep in his throat. His mouth worked as he chewed, and she couldn't look away, not when he licked an errant crumb from the side of his mouth, not when he swallowed the moist dessert, not when he drew in a deep breath to speak again.

"It's very good," he said.

Elle swallowed thickly. *Yeah.* She cleared her

throat once, then twice. "Does this mean you're a convert to sweets?"

"This one is definitely growing on me," he said.

Drawing in a shuddering breath, Elle retreated back to her side of the table. Her hand, she noticed, was shaking. "You did that to me on purpose."

His eyes were pools of wicked desire. "Me? Never."

"God… I feel like I'm about to slide right off this chair and into your lap," Elle murmured, impossibly turned on and nearly shameless from it.

"If you two are done having eye sex, is there anything else in the case I can get for you?" Carole appeared at their table, apparently done with the wedding-cake women.

She stood with her hands on her hips, looking down at them with a maternal look that should have been out of place on her young face but somehow wasn't.

"Yes," Ahmed said without looking away from Elle's fiercely blushing cheeks. "A dozen of the red velvet cupcakes, please. Actually, make that two dozen, one dozen per box."

"Let me guess, one box is for Elle?"

He looked away from Elle with a soft laugh. "You see right through me."

Carole giggled, obviously loving the whole situation, especially since she was getting a big sale out of it. Elle was only grateful that with the sound of the radio along with the other humming noises in the small bakery, her earlier words had mostly been muffled. "Two dozen red velvet cupcakes coming right up. It's a good thing I have some extra in the back." Then she left.

"Oh, God." Elle felt like burying her face in her hands but *just* restrained herself from doing something so dramatic. "I probably won't be able to show my face in here again."

"I doubt that. She likes you and your business." He brushed her hand lying uselessly on the table next to her half-devoured cupcake. "Besides, you have nothing to be embarrassed about."

Then he picked up the cupcake with the imprint of his teeth and devoured it in two bites. He licked his lips after it was all gone. "This is a taste I can definitely get used to," Ahmed said.

After they finished their coffees and settled up the bill with Carole, he walked her out of the shop, following closely behind her with the pastry boxes deftly balanced in one hand.

"Let me walk you to your car," he said.

Because it was a busy Sunday in the trendy neighborhood, Elle had had to park on a side street. "I'm that way. It's a little far," she cautioned.

"I don't mind. My legs work just fine. Come on."

Their steps synchronized on the uneven brick sidewalk.

"I hope I didn't embarrass you too much back there," he said.

A breath of laughter left her mouth. "I thought you said there was nothing to be embarrassed about?"

"That's what I think, but I know you have your own very strong mind about things."

Elle could still feel the heat in her cheeks from their blatant flirtation, a flirtation she'd allowed to power along on all cylinders until she remembered that Carole was watching along with anyone else in the bakery with even a little curiosity. She'd never been an exhibitionist and didn't intend to start being one now that Ahmed was... Her brain stuttered. Exactly what was he? And what was she doing with him?

She was so distracted by the dilemma of him that she almost walked past her car.

"This is me." Face flaming, she took a few steps back on the sidewalk until the driver's-side door of her little green Audi was at her hip.

"This isn't too far," he said. "From what you said, I thought we'd be walking all the way to Midtown."

"Close enough," she said, although the walk had felt short to her, too. Elle took her keys from her purse, proud that her hands were absolutely *not* shaking. "Okay. I guess I better get going."

"If you have to. But I could stand here with you all day."

She laughed at his foolishness. "Doing what?" she asked, although she felt pretty much the same thing. Their conversation had been surprisingly easy, their flirtation fun and some of the best foreplay she'd had in months. Elle's core clenched at the thought, and she turned her back to the car, the sun-warmed body of the vehicle pressing into her butt and thighs through the slacks when Ahmed reached up to put the boxes on top of the car.

"Here, let me."

He took the keys from her and clicked open the car door, slid one of the pastry boxes into the passenger seat, and straightened back to his full and impressive height.

"Thank you for having coffee with me," he said. "And for introducing me to something sweet I can sink my...teeth into."

Despite her resolution not to let Ahmed rattle her in any way, Elle felt her face heat again. This was getting out of control. "I need to get in my car and go before you get me accused of public indecency."

He chuckled, his voice low and sexy as it rumbled from deep in his chest. "I'm surprised at you, Princess Elle." And this time, there was no twist of cynicism to his mouth when he called her that. "None of that was even close to threatening the public's decency." As he spoke, he moved closer until his big body was crowding her against the car, and Elle was breathing in a deep lungful of his intoxicating scent. Faintly smiling, he dipped his head and showed her what a real threat to public decency felt like.

Elle trembled at the brush of his warm breath over her lips. He settled his big hands on her waist and moved close enough for her to feel the firm line of his belly against her own.

"Will you let me in, princess?"

Her breath trembled out, and she breathed him in. "Yes."

Ahmed pressed the gorgeous line of his mouth against hers. Heat. Firmness. A delicious pressure that weakened her. Elle braced her palms against his belly, trying to find something to steady her shifting world, but she ended up gripping his shirt, her fingers digging into the soft material over his hard flesh while his mouth brushed hers.

She groaned into his mouth as their tongues touched, a delicious wet stroke that made her panties feel abruptly tighter. She opened up for him, gasping when he sucked gently on her tongue and licked the damp insides of her mouth, making her whimper in delirious pleasure.

He didn't play fair. Ahmed caged her against the car with the hard furnace of his body while his hands on her hips grounded her against him——his hands all that prevented her from flying away. The slow stroke of his tongue was sinuous and hot, conjuring the stroke of other things, waking up every bit of her body, setting her lips tingling.

Wow, he was good at this. So good.

And his scorching kisses made her wonder what else he might be good at. Made her gasp and moan into his mouth and strain to get closer to his heat, her legs falling open and making her grateful she'd worn pants so she could feel the hard inches pushing rhythmically against her.

*Oh, God...*

She stood on her tiptoes to get more of him. He cursed into her mouth, groaning.

"We should stop... We should..." But his hips

ground into hers, and she felt just how much he didn't want to stop. And she was just far gone enough to—
He pulled away from her, their lips parting with a wet noise.

"Jesus!" he growled into her throat, and he leaned heavily into her, nearly crushing her with the heady heat of his body. "I'm this close to climbing into the back seat of your tiny car," he rumbled into her skin.

Elle shook herself. No. This wasn't something she did. Ever.

But she greedily reached for him again despite knowing better, their mouths latching together again. It was another long moment before they pulled apart.

"I really hadn't planned on having sex with you in the middle of Grant Park, Elle. But I'm a weak man." He pressed his hips into hers again and they both groaned.

Elle flushed. She stepped away from him and delicately wiped the corners her mouth with trembling fingers. An invitation for him to come with her to her bedroom hovered just a breath away.

"Do you have somewhere you want to be?" he asked, his voice rasping and deep.

She shook her head.

"I know a place. A hotel." He sounded nearly as desperate as she felt. But then the meaning of his words washed over her. A hotel. If he'd asked her to go home with him, she probably wouldn't have hesitated, probably would have broken every speeding law in Atlanta to get there and be waiting naked on the bed when he locked the door behind them.

But this…this was like an invitation to be one of his throwaway women. And she didn't even realize what that meant until she was shaking her head.

"I'm sorry," he said with a wry twist of his mouth. "That…" He took a deep breath and looked regretful. "That came out wrong."

"It probably came out exactly the right way." Elle crossed her arms and clutched at her own sides, suddenly cold. She wasn't exactly holding out for marriage, but she wasn't on the level of Shaye and other women she knew who could have sex without any emotional consequences. She wanted Ahmed Clark. And it meant something. "I, um, I'm going to head home."

Ahmed reached out to touch her, seemed to change his mind at the last minute and braced his hand against the roof of her car instead.

"I don't have my head so far up my ass that I don't know what that means."

Elle couldn't think of anything to say that wouldn't make this more awkward. Ahmed pulled away from her, withdrawing the last of his body heat, and left her trembling against the door of her car.

"Okay," he said, then lightly touched the face of his watch. "I should get going to…to take care of something." His trembling voice spoke volumes, told Elle he was just as rocked by this attraction between them as she was.

It felt good to know she wasn't the only one in this. Even if Ahmed just wanted to get his rocks off with her in a hotel room then forget about her before the sheets were even cool. "Okay," she said.

"I want to call you," he said, surprising her. "Can I?"

Elle may have been back to standing on both feet but she still felt off balance with him, uncertain in ways she hadn't been since she was a teenager. "Um…sure."

"Good." He backed away and took his box of pastries from the roof of her car and strategically held it low in front of him. "I'll talk with you later."

"Yes. Later."

She climbed into her car and started it then sat behind the wheel with her turn signal clicking and watched Ahmed walk away, hypnotized by the promise in the wide-legged roll of his hips. Even in the loose jeans, the muscles and thickness of his butt were obvious, the flesh hard and meaty enough for her to sink her nails into while he—

A car horn honked just behind her, yanking her mind out of the gutter. A VW Beetle waited impatiently to get into her parking spot. Elle fumbled for the gearshift and pulled out of the parking space, maneuvering onto the street and somehow making it home without getting into an accident. It was a minor miracle.

## Chapter 10

The social change and activism conference after-party was lit. Strobe lights flashed over the cordoned-off dance floor while Rihanna encouraged the already sweaty dancers to *work, work, work, work, work* from the bass-thumping speakers. Conversation tripped through the room and everybody was gorgeous. Elle stood back with her glass of champagne while Shaye sashayed around the hotel ballroom in her emerald green dress and high heels.

Like most people at the party, Shaye was there for networking and coalition building for one of the many social-justice organizations she was a member of. Comfortable in jeans and T-shirt during the day—or at least Shaye's version of that normally tame out-fit—her best friend had now pulled out all the stops in her short and tight designer dress to flirt, seduce and drink the night away. These activists worked hard in the trenches day and night, but when it was time to party, they *partied*.

Occasionally drinking from her glass of champagne, Elle enjoyed watching the crowd of intense and intensely beautiful people. Their energy was amazing. She didn't know where they got it from, the strength to constantly push back against a system fighting to keep people uneducated and unaware.

At times like these, she had nothing but respectful awe for people like Ahmed and Shaye. They did the work that frightened her. Work she was only happy to support with her checkbook.

"Oh, excuse me!" A pretty woman in a dress tight enough to rival the one Shaye wore bumped into Elle and spilled the cool champagne over her hand and the hem of her black dress.

Elle jumped back from the splash of alcohol with a soft cry. At least it wasn't red wine. "It's okay," she said. "It won't stain."

"I'm glad," the woman said. "It would be a shame to ruin such a pretty Valentino. Those rent-a-couture places don't take kindly to messed-up merchandise." Then, with that parting shot, the woman dashed off into the crowd, her big behind wiggling for all it was worth in her flame-red dress.

*What the...?*

"Well, that's a booty for you." Shaye materialized at Elle's side.

"Yeah, and a bitch, too." She frowned after the

woman who'd assumed she didn't own the vintage designer dress she wore. Then, with a roll of her eyes, she shrugged off the stranger's comment to focus on what Shaye said about her butt.

"Do you think it's all hers?"

"Yeah," Shaye said with a snort of laughter. "I'm sure she paid for it somehow."

They leaned into each other, giggling.

On the other side of the room, the big-butt woman was flirting with a massive guy in a sport coat and slacks. He looked like a football player.

"Are you good?" Shaye looped her arm around Elle's waist.

Elle was there as her friend's plus-one. And Shaye had been a great date so far, making sure Elle enjoyed herself even though she didn't know many people at the party. But Elle *was* having fun. The people-watching action was prime.

"I'm good, girl. Just keep having fun. Don't worry about me." But she might as well have told the sun not to shine.

"When have I ever not worried about you?" Shaye tugged at Elle's waist. "Come and taste this mini souf-flé thing. It's amazing. I don't even know how they did it."

Shaye dragged Elle over to the table with the apparently miraculous tiny soufflés, her arm still draped around Elle's waist to prevent her from escaping to another corner. The little appetizers did turn out to be good.

"Okay, not bad," Elle conceded after she bit into

the second one and nearly moaned out loud at the perfectly light concoction and its both sweet and tart weight on her tongue.

"Great, because if you disagree with me on this, I'm not sure we could still be friends." Shaye teased her with a bump of her hip.

Shaye reached for another soufflé, and Elle narrowed her eyes at her friend, wondering why Shaye was spending time with her when she could be flirting with other passionate activist types.

"What's up?" Elle asked and backed out of the way of a slim guy approaching the hors d'oeuvres with single-minded determination. She kept an eye on the dwindling supply of soufflés but most of her attention on Shaye.

Her friend shrugged. "The usual. There's a guy…"

"Of course." Elle laughed but felt there was more going on. "You playing hard to get?"

"Please. When have I ever?" Shaye giggled like that was the funniest thing in the world. "He's not sure." She leaned in to whisper, "He's young, so I'm giving him some space to figure out whether or not he wants to dip his wick with me tonight."

"There isn't anything else?"

Shaye shrugged. "Just massaging a few contacts to see about getting into that policy meeting at the White House next month. They have rumors about actually changing the laws to give us what we need, but you know…"

Rumors like this usually meant nothing if the people enacting them were still unwilling to treat others fairly. "Yeah, I know."

Shaye slid a hand through the ends of her thick curls, sighing. Sometimes she carried such hope for a better world that Elle worried for her. Unlike Elle, who freely embraced her own pessimism, Shaye was the perennial optimist. Because of that, the world was destined to break Shaye's heart. For a moment, even with the lights of the ballroom chandeliers glittering over her beautiful face and eyes, she looked exhausted.

"Things will work out, Shaye. Maybe not for the best, at least not right now, but they'll still be okay."

Shaye closed her eyes and looked almost embarrassed that she might have allowed her real feelings to show to anyone else around them, and then she leaned into Elle with the scent of her crisp and sweet perfume floating around them. "Thanks, babe." Another sigh rippled through her long body.

Seconds later, Shaye straightened, squeaking with excitement. "Did you know he was here?"

"Who?" When Shaye didn't respond, Elle pulled back and turned around to see who she was talking about.

Of course, it was Ahmed. She bit the inside of her cheek.

And…wow.

The day she saw him in person for the first time, Ahmed had just about knocked her over with his gorgeous looks. And he'd only been wearing street clothes—jeans, button-up and a blazer. Now, though, he was positively edible in a sleek dark suit, complete with tie, a pocket square and even a tiepin. Unlike his usual casually refined looks, tonight's outfit screamed money.

"I guess you *didn't* know," Shaye said with a pleased sigh.

"What?"

"You should see your face right now. You look like you want to run across the room and jump on him."

What would he do if she did? Elle idly wondered then nearly stumbled after the thought careened through her brain, leaving chaos in its wake. Since he was in such great shape, she knew he could easily take her weight, would barely rock back on his heels if she climbed him, wound her arms around his neck, her legs—

"Um…no."

"That wasn't very convincing." Shaye laughed, fingers fluttering up to cover her mouth. "You should try again. Or, better yet, get over there, and make him notice how sexy you look tonight."

Sexy? Elle looked down at the relatively simple black designer dress that bared her shoulders and hugged her body to the waist, with a peacock's ruffle low at her hips that enhanced her behind. The dress was serving full Dorothy Dandridge as Carmen Jones—complete with a red flower in her hair—and was the outfit Shaye picked for her to wear tonight. *Wait a minute…*

"Did *you* know he'd be here?"

"No comment." But Shaye cackled, giving herself

away. She gave her empty plate to a passing waiter and brushed her hands off as if her work was done.

"I don't think this is a good idea, Shaye. Ahmed is..." Elle didn't even know how to finish that sentence.

After they saw each other at The Baked Good, he'd called her like he said he would, but between her schedule and his, they'd barely managed to exchange anything meaningful. But there had always been the promise of more, and later, and *soon*.

"What he *is* is interested in you. And you're into him, too. What else is there to say?" Shaye bumped her hip again. "Go over there and talk to him. It can't hurt."

She jerked her chin toward Ahmed, who hadn't stopped looking mouthwatering in the few minutes Elle had taken her eyes off him.

Elle raised her eyebrow. "Have you met me?" Shaye knew better than anyone how Elle had fought in foster care against some of the very people who were supposed to take care of her. She knew how those experiences affected how Elle shared her body and with whom.

"It doesn't have to be a casual thing, sweetie. It might become more. You never know."

Elle shook her head, denying the optimism her friend spouted. But she couldn't stop staring at Ahmed.

He stood in a loose circle of other athletic-looking men, hands in the pockets of his well-fitting slacks, casually mouthwatering in a way that should've made most of the other men in the room rethink their fashion choices.

God, she felt so stupidly gone over him.

"Come on!" Shaye said, apparently at the end of her patience. "If you're not going to mosey on over there on your own, I might as well drag you."

But before Shaye could follow through with the threat, the woman who'd bumped Elle's arm and spilled champagne over her appeared at Ahmed's side.

He didn't touch the woman, but she touched him, a casual caress of his arm that spoke to an old and intimate relationship. His strong body straightened to tower over the voluptuous woman's petite frame, and his bright teeth flashed. It looked like she was trying to pick him up, and he was letting her.

"Oh," Shaye said. "Maybe we won't go over there right now." A look of apology twisted her face.

"Yeah. That's probably for the best." Elle didn't want to dwell on the disappointment that turned the soufflés to lead in her stomach.

With determined cheer, Shaye snagged a couple of glasses of champagne and turned them toward the opposite side of the room. "Let's go see what my night's would-be boyfriend is up to."

"Okay. That sounds like a good idea." Or at least a distracting one.

They wove their way through the crowded ballroom with Shaye occasionally pausing to greet this person or that, her smile of welcome never wavering even while she pushed them steadily away from Ahmed and the woman who would most likely take him home for the night.

Elle swallowed the lump in her throat and pinned

on a smile. It took them only a few minutes to find Shaye's indecisive boy and less time than that for him to make up his mind that he wanted Shaye.

Elle left her friend to her evening seduction and drifted into a conversation with a popular news anchor who'd just become the subject of the news herself when her husband got caught with a notorious escort.

The anchorwoman, Treah McConnell, didn't mention the escort incident and neither did Elle, even though she knew Shaye was dying to know all the behind-the-scenes details.

"I did hear about your business," Treah was saying. "My brother could really use your services. He's hopeless at planning outings for his wife, but he still wants to make her happy."

"Wanting to please the person you're romancing is the first step toward a successful date," Elle said, taking out one of her business cards. "Pass this on to him. Romance Perfected would be more than happy to help him and his wife create an evening both of them can enjoy."

"If having the desire to please your lover was a guarantee of good results, the world would be a much happier place." A low voice rumbled just behind Elle, sending a shiver of reaction through her body. She turned to face Ahmed.

"It's the first step," she said. "Not the entire journey."

He had the nerve to grin down at her as if he wasn't about to take another woman to bed at the end of the night. He passed his good cheer around, greeting Treah and begging her pardon for interrupting.

"No pardons necessary," Treah said with an indulgent look between Elle and Ahmed. "You two probably have a lot to talk about anyway, and I'm never one to stand in the way of romance."

"We don't have a—" *romance*. But Treah was already stepping away to talk with someone else.

"Why do you always know the exact *wrong* to say?" Elle narrowed her eyes at him, allowing her irritation to show.

"Put your claws back in, kitten. I'm only here to say hello." The corners of his mouth curved up, and his gaze moved down, devouring her from red flower to black stilettos. "And to tell you how gorgeous you look."

Elle wanted to punch him. "Thank you. I think. Won't your...lady of the evening object to you telling another woman how nice she looks?"

"Who's my lady?" He made a show of looking around the room.

Elle sucked her teeth, although it was mostly in irritation at herself. Now he knew she'd been watching him. "That woman in the red dress who was practically drooling in your crotch."

His eyebrows flew up then he laughed. "That's a very vivid description and also very wrong." He laughed even more, a masculine rumble of sound that drew more than a few appreciative looks his way. When she didn't join in on the laughter, his humor trickled away though it didn't completely stop. "You're jealous."

"Absolutely not," Elle said. But she'd never been a good liar.

Without looking, she could feel his disbelief and his strange…affection.

Elle shifted under his smiling regard. "Stop it. People are looking at us." What exactly she wanted him to stop doing, she couldn't say with any certainty. Whatever it was made awareness prickle all over her body. And drew even more stares. Of course, these people watching them probably all listened to his damn radio show.

"There's nothing to be jealous of, Elle." He stepped closer to her, and she smelled a hint of his aftershave, something crisp and citrusy. "You're the only princess I'm interested in tonight."

"And what about non-princesses?" she asked before she could bite her own tongue off.

He chuckled, another low and sensual sound. "You're the woman I want right now. I think you know that."

Well, she knew he *said* it. She was naive about certain things, but a man declaring his singular interest while his libido was piqued wasn't one of them.

She crossed her arms over her chest and cocked her hip. "If that's true, prove it."

Ahmed's eyes darkened as they slowly moved down her body. "For some reason, you seem intent on getting me locked up on some sort of public indecency charge."

Elle clenched her jaw and willed herself not to blush at the blatant reminder of what had happened between them when he walked her to her car a few days before. Her will was apparently weak where he was concerned.

"That's not what I'm talking about," she said finally.

"Then what do you mean? What other proof do you need to believe that I want you tonight in my bed or anyplace you'll have me?"

Elle's face wasn't getting back to its normal temperature anytime soon, apparently. She pressed a hand to her cheek and looked anywhere but at his face, or the open collar of his shirt, or anywhere on his body. Her wandering eyes found Shaye, and her friend gave her the thumbs-up then changed it to the "call me later" sign with her thumb and index finger held near her face like a telephone. She was leaving with her boy toy. Good for her.

Elle refused to be jealous that Shaye did whatever she wanted and never seemed to second-guess herself. A hand on her waist brought her attention firmly back to Ahmed. He looked worried, a complete reversal of the hungry look he'd worn moments before. "I feel like I'm always apologizing to you," he said.

"What...?"

"I'm apologizing now, at any rate. I don't want you to feel pressured. I want you, I want to make love to you in any way you'll let me, but only when and if you're ready."

"I..." She wasn't ready. Or was she? Everything

inside her throbbed an enthusiastic "yes," but slinking off to sleep with gorgeous men she'd barely known for a month wasn't her style. She toyed with the diamonds in her ears.

"Tell you what? Let's just have a nice time tonight," Ahmed said softly. "I'll introduce you to a few colleagues of mine. Maybe get some business thrown your way. No pressure. No sex talk." His hand hovered near her waist, not touching but not moving away either. It was torture. "What do you say?"

Business. Yes, she'd come here for business with Shaye. Her partner could swan off with her "boyfriend of the evening," but Elle still had a job do. She'd only had two motives coming to this party: to be Shaye's plus-one and to drum up clients for Romance Perfected. With a little over a week to go until Valentine's Day, this was the perfect time and place to give out her card. But…she wanted to be reckless. She wanted to say *yes* to Ahmed and let him take her to the nearest bed.

"Okay." Elle was very aware of how close Ahmed was to her, aware of the loose circle of his arm near her waist that was an odd sort of corral, turning her where he wanted without actually touching her, a clear indication that he *wanted* to touch her but didn't dare.

She ached for that caress.

"Let's go sell some romance." Elle clapped her hands once and managed to dredge up a smile.

For the rest of the evening, she kept to his side as he introduced her to his friends and colleagues in the activist, sports and celebrity communities. They joked with Ahmed and teased Elle for allowing a player like him to take her out. They all seemed to genuinely like him. By the end of the night, she'd passed out all her business cards and sent the website details for Romance Perfected to more than one smartphone.

The only hiccup had come when the champagne-spilling girl in the red dress came up to Ahmed wearing a pout.

She interrupted as he was reassuring a friend and former teammate that he *would* keep sending controversial tweets to stir up the haters and prod the people who were still deeply asleep instead of being "woke."

"Ahmed, baby." The woman's voice was much sweeter than when she'd talked to Elle. "I'd love to get your new number before I leave here. Like I said earlier, it's been far too long and we should catch up." She pressed close enough that her breasts pushed into his arm, and Elle had to clench her hands behind her back to stop herself from wrenching the woman away and dropping her on her fat ass in the middle of the ballroom.

But Ahmed finished what he was saying to the ballplayer, not even turning to look at the woman when his friend just about dropped his eyeballs into the woman's cleavage.

"Christine." There was no trace of warmth in his voice, merely polite interest. Barely. "There's no 'catching up' that we need to do." He jerked up his sleeve to look at his watch then briefly touched it. "Would you like a ride home?" he asked Elle.

And Elle quickly swallowed to stop the immediate "yes" from flying out of her mouth. If he took her home, she wasn't sure she'd want him to leave. Not until the morning anyway.

Even with the Christine woman standing there, Elle couldn't do it.

"Thanks for offering," she said instead. "But I have my car here."

Ahmed didn't hide his disappointment. "Maybe next time."

"After your next date maybe?" his friend suggested with a teasing laugh, and Elle could've kissed him because Christine looked like she'd swallowed her tongue. Surprise was not an attractive look on her.

All in all, the night was a success.

But why did she feel like she'd badly failed when she walked into her empty house alone later that night?

After turning on the living room light, Elle kicked off her shoes and sank into the softness of the sofa. With only the distant hum of the fridge and the purr of the air conditioner, the house felt far too empty. She picked up her phone to text Shaye but paused when she heard a key in the door.

Sometimes she wondered why Shaye even kept her own house when she was over at Elle's place so often.

Moments later, her friend walked in, a smile, loose and relaxed, shaping her mouth, which had been wiped or most likely *kissed* clean of lipstick.

Only the faintest trace of red remained on her slightly swollen-looking mouth. She dropped her purse onto the coffee table, ignoring it when the clasp popped open and the contents spilled over the freshly polished cedar surface. Shaye sat beside Elle.

"I don't know how you can do it," Elle found herself grumbling, jealous suddenly, when she hadn't been in all the years she and Shaye had known each other.

"What?"

"This." She gestured to her loose-limbed contentedness, low-necked dress and the purse she'd thrown on the table with the condom packets spilling out.

"Oh." Shaye curved her lips into her favorite smile. Pleased and happily exhausted. "It's just fun. Sex is easy. It's the other stuff that's hard." She gave Elle's cheek a lazy caress. "How did the rest of the party go? Did you and the basketball stud at least talk?" Shaye toed off her shoes and curled her legs under her, leaning back into the overstuffed sofa to give Elle her full, if sleepy-eyed, attention. "You're already home and here alone, so I assume you didn't rescue Ahmed from the pasture to give him the ride of his life?" She playfully waggled her eyebrows.

Elle fought a blush as she remembered Ahmed talking to Christine. The way the woman had seemed so certain he would give her his number or at least promise to call her, only to have him ask Elle about needing a ride.

"A princess should never drive herself anywhere," he'd teased while walking her to her car. But even that comment didn't dull the electric snap of attraction between them.

"There was no riding happening anywhere near me tonight," Elle said. Not that she didn't want to, obviously.

"Too bad."

"Yeah. Too bad…"

"Do you really mean that?" Shaye's voice was low, thoughtful.

She rested her head on the back of the couch. Despite her sleepy gaze, she looked at Elle like she could see past all her issues to the very real need throbbing beneath her surface denials. "Do you really want that man?"

Elle swallowed. She'd never hidden anything from Shaye. Not the good parts of herself and certainly not the bad. The sexual being inside her craved Ahmed Clark with an unfamiliar hunger that started low in her belly then radiated out until every part of her ached for his touch.

"I do."

"Then take him, honey. You deserve pleasure." Shaye was like the devil on her shoulder in the disguise of an angel, complete with heaven-tousled hair and wide eyes. Her slow wink was sly.

Elle smiled at her in agreement.

# Chapter 11

Ahmed strolled into the kitchen from the garage, keys jinglsing, and flipped the light switch to flood the space with light. He flinched from the sudden brightness, but that didn't slow his footsteps to the fridge. He was starving. Nothing they'd served at the party had been enough to satisfy him.

Nothing except Elle.

And *damn*, how he wanted her.

The hunger from that want growled in him, twisted tight in his belly and lower, leaving him constantly and achingly hard. All night at the party, he'd had to keep his hands in his pants pockets so he wouldn't embarrass himself with his obvious lust. That lust tightened in him even more knowing Elle wanted him, too. It hadn't been plainer than when she showed her jealousy over Christine.

His mouth twisted in contempt at the thought of his greedy ex.

Christine had had the nerve to walk up to him like she hadn't tried to steal his money, trampling his pride and trust in the process. She'd been seductive and friendly, probably putting on a show for her latest victim, but instead of acting on the twin engines of fury and revulsion that nearly drove him to the opposite side of the room from her, Ahmed had stood still while she pawed him, acted like her presence didn't make him want to warn every man in the room to check their wallets and bank accounts for theft. She belonged in jail. Or at least very far away from him.

Ahmed took a piece of roast chicken from the fridge and sat down to eat at the breakfast bar.

Christine's presence had only briefly dimmed his fixation on Elle. Once he'd dismissed her and the overinflated ego she'd ridden in on, Elle was firmly back at the center of his attentions.

He took a bite of a cold chicken leg and chewed slowly in contemplation, not quite ready to name Elle an obsession but very much aware she was close enough to it. And the hunger for her didn't even feel like it was about sex. Well, at least not completely.

Halfway through his late-night snack, Sam lurched into the kitchen looking only a few steps removed from death.

"Where the hell have you been?" his cousin demanded, although his voice was thready and weak, barely above a whisper.

Sam had been sucker punched by crippling migraines over the last few hours, trapped in his bed and unable to deal with even the weakest light or sound. It was good to see him upright again.

"The coalition party downtown." Ahmed pushed the platter of chicken toward the empty seat across from him that his cousin automatically took. "Remember?"

"I *remember* telling you not to go without me."

"And I remember telling you I can take care of myself." Sam had been in no condition to leave the shadowy darkness of his room much less shadow Ahmed to a party filled with bright lights, loud conversation and Ahmed making a fool of himself.

Sam brooded across from him, his mouth drooping and the corners of his eyes tight from strain. Ahmed got up and turned the adjustable overhead lights to their lowest setting without leaving the kitchen completely in the dark. His cousin muttered his thanks then spread his fingers against the granite counter, staring at the slight tremor in them.

"Christ…"

Ahmed knew better than to ask Sam if he was okay. His cousin was double listed in the dictionary under *stubborn* and *self-sufficient*. PTSD and occasional migraines took their toll on him on an all-too-frequent basis, but he was determined to function as close to normal as possible. It had taken a near miracle to have him agree to live in the pool house, and he only did that because he insisted on paying Ahmed rent.

Eventually, Sam got himself together to start scolding Ahmed again.

"You don't know what people will do." Then he stopped and squinted at Ahmed, leaning close. "Did you see that woman? Elle Marshall?" Sam sat back on the stool. "Actually, you don't even need to answer that. I can practically smell her all over you."

"Don't be creepy, Sam."

"I can't help it," he said, his voice sounding stronger now that he had a cause to fight for. "It's in my job description."

Technically, he had no job description except to keep Ahmed safe from outside threats; what Ahmed did to himself was entirely his own responsibility.

"That wasn't smart. You don't know what or who is out there waiting for you—or me—to mess up."

"Like those reporters from the other day? That was just Clive being a manipulative bastard. After my date with Elle, they lost interest. I can't speak for what'll happen at the radio station tomorrow, though." Once he was back on the air and Clive decided what other crazy stunt he was going to pull, who knew what the audience reaction would be?

"So what happened with Princess Elle?" Sam asked.

Ahmed shrugged and went back to eating his cold chicken. "I'm sure you already have some idea, since your sense of smell is working so well."

"You slept with her? Already?"

"No!" Although he would've been doing that right now if not for Elle's good sense. He finished chewing and swallowed the small bite. "She told me no."

"That's good. I'm glad one of you is thinking clearly. You don't need to get involved with someone we haven't vetted."

Ahmed froze. "Are you for real? Weren't you the one telling me to give a chance and be nicer to her? Where was all this coming from?"

"Being nice doesn't mean having sex with her. Every other day, you act like you're the one of us with PTSD when a pretty woman comes near. You grab your wallet like she's going to take you for everything you've got."

Even though his cousin was exaggerating, Sam reminded Ahmed of the reasons he didn't get involved with women whose agenda he wasn't sure of up-front. He'd gotten hurt in the past not checking things out and only had himself to blame for being so damn naive. But he wasn't a rookie ballplayer anymore. He didn't have that excuse.

He liked Elle, though. She was firmly under his skin. One date and two unplanned encounters later, he was already thinking of when he could see her again. And just how far they would take their...acquaintance.

Their flirtation was electric, and despite her reluctance to fall into the nearest available bed with him, he knew she wanted the same thing he did—her gasping his name, writhing beneath him in a bedroom thick with the smell of sex and impending satisfaction.

But Sam was right. Ahmed couldn't be irresponsible about this. Seeing Christine again made that point all too clear.

"Fine," Ahmed said. "Do what you need to, but don't invade Elle's privacy." Was that even possible given the means Sam had at his disposal?

"Cool." Sam's face settled into lines of calm now that he had a purpose, the signs of strain and discomfort nearly erased.

"And don't break any laws while you're at it," Ahmed muttered.

Sam gave a mock salute, a much more restrained one than usual, before slipping quietly from the kitchen.

With his cousin gone, Ahmed reached for his food again, but his phone vibrated on the countertop, loud and insistent, before he could put anything in his mouth.

"Hello?" A soft breath came at him through the line. He glanced down at the caller ID. "Elle?"

"I…I want to see you," she said.

And just like that, he was back in his fantasy of her in his bed, straining toward her pleasure under him. She breathed into the phone again, a soft and trembling noise that rushed any remaining blood above his shoulders fully south.

"Come to my house." His hand clenched into a fist near the forgotten platter of food, a useless effort to stem the tide of lust rolling through him. "Can you?"

"What's your address?"

Ahmed breathed deeply, evenly. When he could

speak again, he gave her the address and the code to get through the gate.

"I'll meet you at my front door," he said, quickly thinking about the journey she would have to take up the winding drive to the mansion, the circular drive-way, the marble steps.

"In an hour," she said.

"Okay."

After he hung up, he didn't know what to do with himself. The conversation replayed itself in his mind, her tone of voice, the excitement galloping through his veins. Ahmed took a breath then another until he was as close to calm as he was going to get. He hadn't felt this worked up about a woman since he was a teenager. Damn, maybe never.

What was the big deal, though? It was a hookup. Nothing he hadn't done before.

Except he'd never invited a woman to his home before, not for sex. And certainly never someone like Elle.

Before the hour was up, he took a shower, made sure his family stayed as far away as possible by send-ing a few subtle texts and making a couple of calls. When Elle rang the doorbell, he was already back in the kitchen, nervously tabbing between his social media pages on his phone.

He wiped his slightly damp palms on his thighs before opening the door.

"Hey," he muttered like an idiot and stared.

Elle had changed from the sexy little black dress into something less formal—another dress, a pale pink thing that shimmered against her chestnut skin and reminded him of the morning they first met. The dress flared out around her slender thighs and hips, the high waist drawing attention to her subtly hourglass shape and the curve of her small breasts under the close-fitting fabric. She was absolutely gorgeous, but that wasn't why he stared. Elle carried a small bunch of red and white tulips.

This was different. "Are those for me?" Ahmed asked with a grin.

"Yeah. I figured this would feel less like a typical booty call if one of us brought flowers. Since I'm the one coming to your house, it might as well be me." She thrust the flowers at him, a shy smile curving her lips.

"They're nice." Ahmed damn near didn't know what to say. This was the first time a woman, or anyone, had brought him flowers. The bright red-and-white blooms *were* nice, but the gesture was even more so.

"I have to admit—" she said with the flowers still held out "—I feel a little silly with them."

Ahmed grasped her hand with the flowers but didn't take the blooms from her.

"Women with flowers are never silly." And he brought her hand, flowers and all, to his lips. He kissed her knuckles. One by one.

The softest of sighs left her mouth, and she whispered his name. Her inhibited response took him by surprise and sparked an answering warmth deep in his belly.

He kept going. Kissing her fingers, the smell of the

flowers took over his senses, the stems firm under the brush of his fingers and the petals velvety when they touched his cheek. Her skin was just as soft, faintly salty and incredibly addictive. Ahmed kissed the back of her hand, her wrist. Elle sighed again and the sound went straight to his groin.

Damn, she was sexy.

He took her other hand, kissed its palm and sucked one of her fingers into his mouth. She gasped again, and she dropped the flowers, the faint sound of them tumbling to the floor like a dress falling from soft shoulders. He groaned and sucked her finger deeper, watched from beneath his lashes as her lips fell open on a whimpering moan. She stumbled back, but the wall stopped her fall, and Ahmed followed with his body, still sucking and kissing her finger, which smelled like flowers.

"What are you doing?" She breathed the question, her voice barely audible.

"Giving you a proper welcome to my home."

Elle licked her lips, her lashes low over lust-glazed eyes. "I think—" Then she gasped when he nipped the center of her palm with his teeth.

"Yes?" He teased her, although he was far gone himself, desperate enough to have her that the bulge in his pants was damn near obscene.

Breathless, Elle tried again. "Someone might… might come." And the sound of her broken voice made Ahmed want to wreck her even more.

"Hopefully, it'll be one of us." And he sank to his knees.

He'd never been so grateful for a dress in his life. Ahmed pressed his face into her lap, searching for the scent of her arousal through the layers of cotton, and found it. He shuddered and mouthed at the material over her lap.

"I want to taste you," he growled, hands already diving under her dress to get at what he suddenly craved.

He tugged at her panties, pulled them off and stuffed them into his pants pocket. The smell of her was strong in the room, an earthy scent that made his mouth water.

"Can I put my mouth on you?"

"Yes," she gasped softly, her head dropping back against the wall with a soft thud.

She whispered the word again and he tasted her wetness with his fingers, stroking the firm pearl of her pleasure. Her thighs fell open even more, gifting him with more of her rich and salty scent. A hitching and moaning breath. Her fingernails sank like delicate little teeth into the back of his neck. Then he put his mouth at the source of her pleasure, and he received the gift of one of the sweetest sounds in the world, the low moan of his name on her lips.

*So sweet...*

He hummed in pleasure, flattening his tongue to lick and taste her, drinking up the salt-laced wine of her sex and the aural ambrosia of her soft moans. Elle circled her hips, grinding her center against his mouth, seeking even more pleasure. He gripped her thighs, held them open and dived in for more. He loved it all. The way she moved against him, moaned his name, arched into him, and begged for more. He *ached* with his desire for her. Just from this alone, she could make him explode. At that thought, the pleasure rushed dangerously close, and he had to reach down and grab himself to hold it at bay.

He didn't want to finish. Not yet. He pulled back, kissing the soft insides of her thighs, pulling down her skirt.

"Come to bed with me."

"Yes, please."

He swept her up into his arms and, dimly aware of the crush of tulips under his feet, took her through the house and up the stairs to his bedroom. Behind its closed and locked door, he dropped her on the bed and pulled back to get undressed, but she dragged him back over her, spread her legs and pulled him flush against her.

"I want you *now*," she groaned into his mouth, and Ahmed was lost.

Panting and desperate, he quickly unzipped and dragged off her dress, tossing it aside to tumble somewhere in the room. Elle moved with him, her body sensual and graceful, bare limbs settling around him, eager and soft. Then her mouth was hot under his, panting, while she fumbled to undo his belt and zipper, drag his pants and boxer briefs just low enough to bare him to her gaze.

"You are so gorgeous," she breathed, and reached for him.

Her hands scorched desire through him, palms hot

on the globes hanging heavily beneath the thickness of his sex. Then on the weeping head of his shaft. *So good...* The breath hitched in his throat, and his hips bucked, thrusting his arousal into her loose grip. Sweat prickled all over his skin.

Trembling in his eagerness, Ahmed crab-walked his hand into his bedside drawer to get a condom. He grabbed one with relief, ripped open the packet and rolled on the rubber with shaking hands, too far gone to bother with taking off his pants or underwear. Lapping at her had brought his need rising to a fever pitch. The lust writhed in him like a living and ravenous thing. He needed to be inside her. He needed for her to come around him, to shower him with her pleasure.

Despite his desperation to sheathe himself inside her, he wanted to make it good for her, too, to pull out her pleasure, taffy slow, and make her want to do this with him again and again. He took a nipple into his mouth, sucked and licked while caressing her other breast, rolling its firm bud between his fingers. She gasped and surged up, her bare flesh searing him through his clothes, the contrast between her nakedness and his covered body achingly arousing. Her thighs flared wider to receive him.

"Elle." He gasped her name and slowly guided himself into her tightness.

They groaned together.

Hot. Wet. Miraculous.

God, he never wanted her to leave.

With a low groan, he pressed his open mouth into

the dampness of her throat, delicious with the taste of sweat and the faintly bitter scent of her perfume. He began to move. An aching slowness that built, growing with the pleasure and the kittenish whimpers she made under him, delicate noises in contrast to the fierce clasp of her thighs around him, the ravenous motion of her hips.

"You're perfect," he gasped as they raced toward the end together.

A drop of sweat fell from his forehead, splashed down her heaving chest. Elle moaned his name again, her sex tight and wet around him, the pleasure tearing through him like flash after flash of lightning. The bed rocked with their movements. The room rang with her delirious cries. Closer. The heat climbed fast in Ahmed, rippling through his body and pushing him closer to the edge. Elle cried out, still moving frantically beneath him, reaching for what she needed. But she wasn't there yet. Ahmed reached down between them to touch her with firm strokes of his thumb. Elle moved faster beneath him and cried out his name.

His control was slipping, the heat gathering low and tight. Pleasure rushed over him in a tsunami, threatening to overcome him. But he didn't want to leave her behind. Ahmed gripped her hips, adjusted the angle of his thrusts inside her.

Elle tore her lips from his and screamed.

*Oh, yes...*

He let go. And allowed himself to fly with her. His body releasing in pulse after pulse of completion.

Minutes or hours or years later, Ahmed dropped

on his back into the sheets, fighting for every breath. Elle draped herself over him, the weight of her body heavy and sweet. The pins had fallen from her hair, and the dark strands fell around her face and down to her shoulders. Some stuck to her cheeks. Panting, she licked her lips and blinked down at him. Sweat matted her eyelashes, and her throat was a glimmering line of damp in the soft bedroom light.

"Tired?" she asked breathlessly.

He was exhausted. Like he'd run two or ten marathons in a row. His back muscles trembled and twitched, and sweat ran down his skin in waves. He wanted nothing more than to sleep. "No." He panted the denial, cupping the curve of her behind, loving the feel of her bottom and how it fit perfectly in hands. "I'm not tired at all."

"Good." She crawled up his body, bringing the hot scent of her female center close to his mouth. She was pink and dripping and beautiful. "Now you can finish what you started downstairs."

She was insatiable. And he loved it.

Despite the faint pulses of sensation from his orgasm still pulsing through him, Ahmed wanted her again. Wanted to please her. His taste buds perked up, already anticipating her taste. Ahmed gripped her parted thighs and kissed her sex, sighing when she gasped and slid closer, the muscles of her thighs twitching against his cheeks. Elle looked down at him. Her face was a study in arousal, lips parted and wet, eyes low and slumberous, the curves of her body bathed in the soft overhead light. She took his damn breath away.

"Closer," he breathed into her dampness. The desperation to have her under his tongue wiped away any lingering exhaustion.

Her soft laugh tapered off in a groan as he licked her in one long motion. Ahmed nuzzled deeper into her sex to get more of her on his tongue. Her pleasure smeared his chin. She moved against his mouth, writhing as he loved her with his tongue, squeezed her beautifully perfect butt, gripped her and pulled her harder against his ravenous mouth.

"Oh, my…" she moaned. "You're so good at this." Her voice fell away in another deep moan, one that vibrated her body on top of him. "So good…"

He licked her harder, sucked the salted-candy lusciousness over and over again until her moans were constant and she was riding his mouth hard, scraping his lips with the fur of her sex, bathing him in her scent, in her pleasure. He blindly reached up, realizing he'd closed his eyes to savor the taste of her, grasped her breasts, squeezed and stroked her nipples, pinched them.

She cried out his name as she came, her silken sex rippling against his mouth, pulsing and pouring sweet nectar into his mouth. Sympathetic pleasure rushed through him. Even with her shout of orgasm, he squeezed and tugged her nipples still, licked her while she shook and gasped on top of him, quivering like a leaf caught in a storm. He only stopped when she arched away from him and pushed his face away, her cries of pleasure transformed into something like pain.

Elle gasped again and slid away from him, falling limply into the rumpled sheets beside him. "I think you might already know this but just in case you don't, you're the MVP."

"It's nice to have my own opinions confirmed," he said, just because she expected him to. He wasn't disappointed when she laughed again, although softer this time.

They sank into silence together, the only sounds the gradual calming of their breaths. Soon enough, Elle gave a sleepy moan and rolled back into Ahmed. She smelled of sex and satisfaction. He deliberately slid against her, savoring the feel of her skin against his, the languorous movements of her body, the way she smiled up at him with the barest motion of her full lips.

Contentment fell over him like an unfamiliar but welcome blanket.

"Spend the night," he murmured.

The words came out of nowhere and surprised him, but he didn't want to take them back.

A heartbeat passed. "I'd love to, but I can't," Elle said, looking truly regretful. She lightly raked her fingers through the hairs on his chest, and he wondered if she could feel how fast his heart was beating. "I have a meeting in the morning before I go to the radio station."

Damn. He must be really gone to have forgotten he

had to be at the radio station for his regular Wednesday-morning time slot.

"Okay. Meet me before then." He wasn't sure why he needed to see her, he just did. Maybe it was to see for himself that what he'd found with her was more than just sex, more than him wanting to feel her gasping and coming apart under him. "For coffee at the Starbucks near the station," he heard himself say from far away, already beginning that quick slide into sleep, but it was suddenly important for him to see her outside of the farce that had brought them together in the first place. "Promise me."

A warm breath brushed against his throat, and he felt her hand float down his chest and settle low on his belly. Although there shouldn't have been anything left of him to respond and although he was tired, his sex twitched. God, if only he were twenty again...

"Okay," Elle softly. "The Starbucks. Nine fifteen."

"Nine fifteen." Ahmed sighed. Then he was gone.

The next time he opened his eyes, the bed beside him was cold, but a note lay on the pillow. The sound that had woken him chimed again. His phone.

After a glance at the screen and a groan at the early hour, he answered the call. "What's up, Sam?" Ahmed dropped back to the pillow with the phone pressed to his ear. He scratched idly at his belly.

"Come to my place." His cousin sounded serious.

"What's going on?"

"I'll tell you when you get here."

Ahmed debated pressing the issue, after all, it was well past 2:00 a.m. and he had to be at the studio in the morning *after* meeting up with Elle. But he sat up and pushed the covers off his overheated skin. "Gimme twenty minutes." The room smelled like sex, and so did he. That wasn't something he wanted to share with his cousin.

He rushed through a shower to meet Sam in the small pool house where he lived.

"What's up?" he asked, walking in wearing hastily pulled on gray sweatpants and a matching hoodie with his hands jammed in the pockets. Since he was going to climb immediately back into bed, he hadn't bothered with underwear.

His cousin sat on the couch of his spartan living room with a laptop open in front of him on the coffee table. "I did that check on Elle Marshall."

Ahmed found himself bristling but held his irritation in check as he sank into the couch next to Sam. "That I never agreed to."

"Then it's a good thing I checked," his cousin said.

"What do you mean?" Ahmed asked with a trickle of alarm. He couldn't be wrong about Elle. "I doubt there's anything out there for you to find out about her. Nothing at the Christine level of messedup anyway."

"Come take a look." Sam turned the computer screen so he could see.

"She said she didn't know that much about you, but look at his." He clicked and Elle's Facebook page came up on a new tab. Her profile picture was one of her grinning fiercely at the camera, a thorny rose clenched between her teeth.

"You're stalking her Facebook?" Sam was usually more thorough than this or at least used more credible sources of proof of whatever he wanted Ahmed to see. "You of all people know that most stuff on social media is fake."

"To a certain extent, but there are certain things you just can't fake. Look." Sam scrolled down the page and clicked on a post someone else had put on her page. "She said she had no idea who you were before the radio spot."

"That's not exactly what she said," Ahmed protested, because her saying that would have been an outright lie. Someone would have to be living under a rock to not know who he was, before or after his retirement. His career had been meteoric in its blaze, the trajectory of his fame compared to Steph Curry or even Michael Jordan. His looks, active social life, the fact that he'd played for Team USA in the Olympics and had a few guest-starring roles in multiple TV shows and movies had essentially seared him into the current common consciousness. His activism earned him another kind of attention, this time one that exposed him to people through their after-dinner news shows and Twitter trending topics.

Elle had known who he was and said as much. She just didn't know the particulars of his life and didn't care to. At least not back when they first met.

Sam impatiently jiggled the mouse, pulling Ahmed's attention back to the open Facebook post. "Here."

On her wall, someone named Paula had posted

a recent photo of Ahmed from *Sports Illustrated*. It was one of those artsy black-and-white shots of him in midair about to dunk the ball. His bare chest and stomach were damp with the appearance of sweat and damn near every muscle in his neck, arms and calves was on display in the sideways shot. The midthigh basketball shorts draped over his butt in a way he doubted they ever had in real life. Another miracle of Photoshop.

This one is rich enough to make all your worries disappear, the Paula person had typed above the photo along with about a dozen eggplant emoji. Plus, you two would make some hella cute babies.

The post was dated a week before he and Elle met. It had nearly fifty likes and just about as many comments. But Ahmed couldn't see where Elle had responded to the post.

"That doesn't mean a damn thing," he said.

Sam shook his head like Ahmed was just being thick. "Maybe this will change your mind."

"What am I supposed to be looking at now, comments from her high-school yearbook?"

But his cousin opened a folder on his laptop and pulled up a set of spreadsheets he shouldn't have had access to.

"Are these the earnings and loss statements from her business?"

"Stop being such an easy mark and take a look. Didn't she tell her business was doing well?" He didn't wait for Ahmed to confirm because he'd been there, and they both remembered her passionate defense of Romance Perfected, its potential for making money and how well it had done before. "Her business is hemorrhaging money. She even filed bankruptcy a couple of years ago. How is it a coincidence that she linked up with you just now? Don't you think she's playing the innocent a little too well?"

"Come on, Sam. This doesn't mean anything," Ahmed said, but the doubts were already crowding in on him. Then he remembered an image that had disturbed him at the party, Christine in her red dress standing behind Elle. In a trick of light and perspective, she had looked like a devil on Elle's shoulder. Or at least a warning sign of what could come.

"She hasn't asked me for anything."

"Other than to create this publicity stunt with you, which, according to traffic on her website, has been sending lots of new business her way. Just in the last few weeks since this whole thing started with you." Sam closed the laptop with a snap. "Think with your big head, cousin. We don't want this to be another Christine situation."

Ahmed winced.

"Damn. Sorry, man." Sam really did look regretful.

But it was too late. Memories of the woman who tried to ruin him financially rushed over Ahmed, drowning out his common sense. Christine had come into his life near the beginning of his career. A sexy, passionate woman who seemed to have the stereotypical "heart of gold." She never saw an animal she didn't care about, a charity she didn't want to donate someone's money to, an orphan she didn't want to see in a real home. Through months of incredible sex and chess-master level mind games, she'd wormed her way into Ahmed's life, gotten his credit card and financial account information then proceeded to wipe him out.

Luckily, his accountant had caught on before she could do any serious financial damage. The other damage was already done, though. Ahmed's trust in women had been completely destroyed. Any women he allowed in his life after that had been there for a specific purpose and only got just *so* close to him before he firmly but gently moved them on from his life.

*Elle is nothing like Christine*, Ahmed thought but could not say out loud. He didn't like how desperate and gullible those words seemed.

Later that morning, he still hadn't managed to say them out loud. Instead, he was caught in a cycle of memories. Christine's smile. The things she'd said that made him trust her. He had been young, only twenty-four years old. But he hadn't been a child.

Awake from his second round of sleep since six o'clock, he called Elle to cancel their Starbucks date but got her voice mail. He didn't leave a message.

Ahmed sat in the kitchen drinking coffee and reading the news on his iPad, aware of time passing, watching the time for the coffee date get closer, then pass. His stomach wrenched with anxiety and regret. On the kitchen counter his phone chimed, but he ignored the sound. He only lifted his head from the iPad when Sam, already dressed to go to the radio station, came into the kitchen to check on him.

"You ready?" Sam asked, looking fit and well rested in one of his favorite black suits, all signs of strain from his struggle with the migraines now gone.

At nine thirty, Ahmed and Sam left the house for the station.

They arrived with just enough time for Ahmed to greet Clive and, ignoring his questions about how the arranged date with Elle went, slip on the mic during the commercial break between the earlier morning show and his.

After the commercial break, he put on his on-air persona, which wasn't very different from his every-day self, except maybe his on-air persona wasn't a coward. He should have at least left Elle a message. Or answered one of the messages he was sure she'd left. But the mistrustful part of him convinced that Elle was doing him wrong didn't even want to talk to her voice mail.

Then she walked into the sound booth.

Elle looked wounded when she saw him, eyes widening in surprise then flinching closed with pain. She actually stopped in the doorway of the sound booth, the skirt of her mint-green dress sweeping back with a force of momentum like wings sweeping up to whisk her out of the room. Then she seemed to force herself to move forward and settle into the chair across from him. She plucked up the headphones but didn't put them on. They were on a commercial break.

"What happened?" she asked, a frown wrinkling her normally smooth brow and making him feel guilty. "I waited at the coffee shop but you never showed. Obviously."

The smile he gave her was dismissive. He knew that but couldn't help himself. "It's complicated," he said, watching the clock count down to when they would go back on the air. "We can talk about it once we're done here."

The frown deepened. He was going to be on the air much longer than her follow-up spot.

"Okay." She drew out the word, her face practically covered in question marks.

Guilt squeezed Ahmed's chest again. The clock quickly counted down. He signaled for her to put on the headset.

"All right, ATL. I'm sure you all remember where we left off with Romance Perfected a couple of weeks ago." He paused dramatically, flicking his glance only briefly Elle's way. "My date with Elle Marshall." The lights on the studio phone flashed. "Yup, already some of you nosy bastards are calling in to get the 411, but before that, don't forget the reason we're doing this. Valentine's Day. The day women get chocolate and the men get laid, am I right, Elle?"

Even though she'd been watching him, Elle looked surprised that he asked her the question. "Um…not exactly, Ahmed."

"If not exactly, Princess Elle, then tell us what this day is supposed to be about."

Just then the studio door opened and Clive walked in. He sat in one of the chairs in the sound booth and put on a headset, obviously getting ready to be on the air. He looked very pleased with himself, which made Ahmed worry about what the man had in store for him and Elle.

Worried or not, he couldn't keep the man from going on air at his own radio station. He breathed out a quiet sigh of resignation.

"Listeners, we have a surprise guest this morning," he said into the microphone. "The station general manager just came into the studio to join us. I get the feeling he's up to something."

Clive turned on his mic. "That's right." His voice was loud and aggressively cheerful, the complete opposite to Elle's purring but prickly tone. "I'm here to ask the question our audience members are dying to know."

Ahmed groaned dramatically. It wasn't entirely faked. "Come on, Clive. We just got here."

"Yeah, and you haven't cut to the chase yet," Clive said. "None of us are getting any younger and since you ditched the reporters on Saturday afternoon— very clever, by the way—you have to tell us if those on-air sparks between you and Elle turned into something even more interesting during the date." Clive looked from Ahmed to Elle with naked curiosity. "I think I'm speaking for our entire listening audience here when I say, tell me *everything*."

A few more red lights on the phone lit up. More people hungry for a piece of what he and Elle had shared.

Tension spiked down Ahmed's back, but he kept his expression neutral. "The date went fine. We ate, we talked, we didn't kill each other. The end."

"Nope!" Clive laughed with easy dismissal. "This is exactly why I wanted to get everything on film. I knew we couldn't count on you to give us the full details." He turned to Elle. "What about you, Ms. Marshall? Anything you have to whet our appetite for more of AhmElle?"

Elle had been watching them in silence, questions still blazing in her eyes, but at this cue from Clive, she cleared her throat and leaned toward the mic. "It was…it was actually a pretty nice date. Very unexpected." The smallest of smiles touched her lips, and her gaze sought Ahmed's, a clear invitation to savor their shared memory of the afternoon they'd spent together.

But he avoided looking her way. Instead, he steeled himself to hear a dismissive and touristy travelogue of Valerian packaged just for the radio. Hurt cut across Elle's features.

Clive ignored their byplay and pushed on with his own agenda. "So your own company, Romance Perfected, surprised you with a curated date experience that you loved?"

Despite his annoyance at the GM, Ahmed was glad Clive had taken over the impromptu interview because he had nothing. With Elle sitting in front of him, he couldn't stop thinking about last night's conversation with Sam. Was she running a game on him? His gut wanted him to dismiss the question as stupid. But *stupid* was what he'd been with Christine all those years ago, choosing to believe what she told him instead of the things his accountant, lawyer and the security-camera video said she'd done.

Elle answered Clive's question. "The package my business partner put together is one of our top-of-the-line…"

With her seductive voice, she conjured the image of an evening at a local French restaurant that sounded nice enough but was obviously not what they did. She talked about the restaurant and its food, admitting she hadn't gone there but guaranteed it would be a spectacular time spent for any couple.

"That sounds like a date anyone, man or woman, would be lucky to get for Valentine's Day," Clive said, barely avoiding sounding smarmy. "Romance Perfected sounds like a sure thing if you don't want to leave the quality of your special moments to chance."

"Thank you, Clive. I like to think so." Elle didn't sound as if she liked anything very much in that moment although the overbright smile would have fooled Ahmed a few days ago. Close on the heels of that thought was the realization he was the reason her smile was fake.

He shifted in his chair. Then resorted to what he often did when he was uncomfortable. He went on the attack.

"That might be a nice package," he said, putting emphasis on the last word. "But that's not where we went, is it?"

He didn't allow her to answer the question. "We actually went somewhere I arranged. And don't you agree it was much better than anything your floundering business could've put together?"

The expression on Elle's face would've killed him dead if he'd allowed himself to feel its venom. "My business is *not* failing," she hissed.

"Of course it's not failing now," he said, working hard to inject an impersonal sneer into his voice. "You being on this show gave Romance Perfected a lot of publicity. But it wasn't doing well before, right?"

Elle stared at him, her eyes burning coals of hurt and confusion. Then anger flickered to life, a flame Ahmed swore he saw ignite just before she opened her mouth to speak.

"If you know anything at all about advertising, you should at least be aware that its purpose is to expose one's services to a potential client base," Elle said with a lashing whip in her voice. "And advertising is the reason I'm on this radio show and it's a service that I'm paying for." She drew herself up stiffly in her chair, her chin high. "You act like I should be shocked and ashamed that I'm getting what I paid for."

The studio was whisper quiet. Ahmed could feel Sam watching him. Kiara, the intern, on the other side of the glass stared into the sound booth at them, her mouth hanging open and her gum in danger of falling out.

*For God's sake...*

Before Ahmed could respond to Elle, Clive jumped in. "What the hell is going on here? I thought you two had a good time on that date."

"That date didn't matter, Clive. She was just using me."

"Using you for what?" Clive asked, his earlier good mood completely gone. "You have a radio show. She has a business. That's it. There was no so-called *using.*"

"Remember when she said she didn't know anything about me? She was lying."

"Why would I lie to you about something like that?" Then her eyes narrowed. "Is this about last night? Did something happen after I left?"

Clive twisted back and forth in his chair to keep both Ahmed and Elle in his line of sight. "Last night?"

"This has nothing to do with last night," Ahmed said quickly. "This is about your honesty. Or your dishonesty."

"Other than your presumption that I knew about you before the radio show, which I might have because you're a little bit famous, how have I lied to you?"

"According to public record, your business is close to failing. And on your Facebook page—"

"My *Facebook* right now? How old are you?" She pushed away from the desk, her eyes glittering with fury and what Ahmed suspected, with a rush of regret, were tears. "You know what? Never mind. This whole thing has been one giant mistake."

With one more scathing look at him, Elle ripped the headphones off and threw them on the desk, where they skidded to the floor, taking a couple of pens and a stack of loose papers with them. She grabbed her

purse and practically ran out. The sound of the door
slamming behind her reverberated throughout the
room. And probably over the airwaves, too.

*Dammit.*

Ahmed sat frozen in his seat, his heart thudding,
a voice inside his head shouting at him to run after
her. He didn't move. He couldn't.

What the hell did he just do?

"Is this an indication of how well your date with
her went?" Clive looked at him with a raised eyebrow.
Despite his pithy question, he looked concerned.

Ahmed didn't have time to entertain him.

He'd spent years on the basketball court improvis-
ing, so he did it again, putting himself on automatic
pilot to finish out the show. Much later, he wouldn't
be able to recall what he said, only that he managed
to keep his listeners entertained until the next sched-
uled commercial break. He kept a smile on his face
despite the anger and uncertainty churning beneath
his surface. He couldn't look at Clive. He couldn't
look at Elle's empty chair. And he sure as hell couldn't
answer any of the calls now lighting up the station's
phones like the Fourth of July.

Sam stood against the wall, silent and unmoving,
but his cousin's eyes had followed Elle when she
left the room. Was that doubt in Sam's face? Ahmed
squeezed the bridge of his nose but kept going, kept
talking. He had a job to do.

When he reluctantly opened the phone lines for
the first caller, the floodgates opened.

"Did you just say all those terrible things to that girl then let her walk away?"

"Why were you so mean to her?"

"Are you just super paranoid?"

"What did she do to you?"

"Did you sleep with her and then basically just curse her out on the radio?"

"Ahmed, you're messing up, man."

The questions and comments just kept coming, one after the other until he finally had to stop taking calls and spend the rest of the show talking politics and current affairs.

When the show finally ended, he quickly gave up his chair to the host of the next show and left the sound booth, Sam moving quickly to catch up with him.

Ahmed didn't get very far. His legs took him just as far as the reception area before giving out. He dropped into one of the couches, emotionally drained. Sam, who'd been his silent sentry against the wall during the entire show, took a seat beside him.

"I think I messed up," Sam said, looking almost as miserable as Ahmed felt.

But Ahmed wouldn't let his cousin take the blame for his own actions. Ahmed was the one who knew Elle, had shared things with her that he shared with no one else, had made love to her in the bed that no other woman had been in. And, even after all that, he was the one who'd publicly eviscerated her with unproven suspicions. That was all on him.

He sighed and scrubbed his hands over his face, squeezing his eyes shut. "We should go home."

The door to the station's lounge banged open. "Good. Your worthless ass is still here." Elle's business partner, Shaye, blocked the door. Her pretty face was all angles today, her normally full lips tight with obvious rage.

"Your big bodyguard wouldn't be able to stop me from punching you in the face right now." The shell-pink suit she wore might as well have been a suit of armor, the cell phone she clenched in one hand a sword.

Sam immediately went on the alert, standing up and pushing Ahmed behind him. "Step away, miss," he growled.

But Ahmed could see Shaye was no threat, at least not a physical one.

A door opened behind them, footsteps rushed toward them from a nearby office. Within moments, four then six people had poured from other offices and stood at the edges of the reception area to watch the drama unfold. Face hot, Ahmed clenched his teeth. He hated airing dirty laundry in public.

Shaye didn't back down when faced with Sam's threatening bulk. If anything, she looked even more determined to say what was on her mind. Hands on her hips, she walked toward him, her eyes snapping and high heels stabbing the tile like she wished it was some part of Ahmed's body. She looked nothing like Elle, didn't act like her either, but there was something about the way she confronted Ahmed and Sam that was very Elle-like, an unexpected and effectively vicious attack in a pretty package.

"What you did was real low," she said, her narrowed eyes spitting fire. "Elle is the best woman you've ever had come into your life. And this is how you treat her?" She stabbed a finger at him. "You don't deserve her. You don't deserve anything good. And to think I actually liked you and encouraged her to give you a chance." Shaye shook head, apparently in mourning for her past stupidity. "Right now, I'm so damn sorry I pushed her to go on your stupid show. This is as much my fault as it is yours."

Although every word she spoke stabbed him where it would hurt the most, Ahmed let Shaye say her piece. It was what he deserved. Sam, though, kept giving the woman concerned looks like he was worried she'd leap across the five feet of tiled flooring separating them and gouge out Ahmed's throat with her high heel.

"At least you showed your true colors now instead of later, when it would hurt Elle more," Shaye finished. Then with one last disgusted look at Ahmed then Sam, she turned and walked back out the door, her mission apparently accomplished.

# Chapter 12

She wasn't going to cry. It wasn't worth it.

Elle clattered into Romance Perfected, her entire body hot with humiliation and her day blasted to hell. Exactly what had changed for Ahmed between last night and this morning?

He acted like he hated her.

Like the passion they'd shared in his bed and the connection they had before meant less than nothing.

Elle felt like an idiot. Within just a few hours, her heart had gone from soaring higher than it ever had before to being battered and bruised, just about destroyed from the abrupt drop to solid ground.

No. This was *not* heartbreak. Just a betrayal.

The sound of low classical music, a soft piano, played over the speakers in the main reception area of the office. Normally the music soothed her but not today. Instead, it reminded her even more of the reason she needed soothing. Ahmed Clark. Her morning at the radio station. Her stupidity in trusting him.

Elle rushed to her office, quickly closing the door behind her and muffling the music. She needed the distraction of work.

At her desk, she glanced through the office calendar and saw that, without talking to her, Shaye had switched all the day's appointments to her own calendar, leaving Elle to do all the behind-the-scenes work that didn't need her to see anybody. She should have been upset, and normally she would be irritated that Shaye was coddling her and treating her like some fragile thing. But now she was just grateful.

Her office phone rang.

"Romance Perfected. Elle speaking."

"Good." The voice on the other end of the line made her wince. "You're just the woman I want to talk to."

Elle didn't want to talk to Clive. His voice was too much of a reminder of what she'd just been through with Ahmed. Then she winced.

*This is business. Get a grip.*

Romance Perfected needed her to keep her head on straight. And Shaye would kill her if she burned this bridge.

"This must be your lucky day then," she said. Trying to inject a smile into her voice and through the phone even though it was a near impossibility. "What can I do for you, Clive?"

"Well, actually, it's what I can do for you." Clive paused as if waiting for Elle to say something, but when she stayed silent, he continued. "We've had a lot of interest in you and Ahmed, as you already know. And since Valentine's Day is coming up and this interest generated is good for both of us, I thought it would be good if you came back on the show and talked again about your business. This time, Ahmed won't be part of the equation."

Her stomach dipped with anxiety at just the thought of going back to the radio station, but she gritted her teeth. "What do you mean?"

"You can come on the nine o'clock show, an hour earlier than Ahmed's," Clive said. "DJ Don Juan will make an ad spot for you."

The refusal hovered on the tip of Elle's tongue. She didn't want to take the chance of seeing Ahmed again, even if it was to help the business.

"Why are you doing this?" she asked, because as nice as Clive had been, a businessman like him didn't do things this expensive for free.

"I already told you, this would benefit both of us. Your business and mine. Plus—" the sound of shifting papers and hushed voices came clearly through the phone "—I feel bad about what happened today. And I know Ahmed does, too."

"What he feels doesn't matter," she said, wishing that was true. "I don't want to see him. What you and I may agree on now has nothing to do with him. And I would appreciate it if you would respect my wish for that."

She clenched her jaw, knowing that Clive might give her pushback and tell her no since Ahmed was his star, and the star always got what he wanted. And he'd gotten her, hadn't he? Had her moaning and begging for him in his bed like a glorified groupie without the benefit of even a backstage pass to ease the burn of the bad memory.

Elle hated her own weakness. Her stupidity. How could she have let him in so easily? How could she have allowed herself to fall so fast when everything pointed to it being a bad idea? But bad idea or not, the fall had already happened, and she just had to pick herself up, dust herself off and carry on like it hadn't just about crippled her. And dammit, her business was affected. The last thing she wanted to do was look at happy couples and help them plan a perfect date.

The pain of what had happened between her and Ahmed was so raw she couldn't imagine looking him in the face. At least not without wanting to punch him in it.

"Are you still here, Elle?"

"Yes, I am." She squeezed the bridge of her nose, wishing she had more options. Wishing…so many things.

"So will you do it?" Clive persisted. "Just for closure's sake?"

*And to make your radio station some money in the process?*

Outside her office, Elle heard the tap of heels on hardwood. Shaye coming back from whatever appointment she'd rushed off to earlier that morning.

*This is business.*

Elle pressed her lips together. She couldn't afford to bail on Romance Perfected just because she'd made a stupid decision then gotten her feelings hurt.

"Okay," she said. "I'll do it."

Clive's pleased laugh came at her through the phone. "Good! You won't regret this."

*I already do.* "Okay."

"We should do it for the next show," Clive said, suddenly all business. "I'll contact you in a few hours with the details."

"That sounds good," Elle replied, although every part of her rebelled against it. When Shaye knocked on her door, she covered the mouthpiece to invite her partner in then went back to the conversation with Clive. "I'll let you know if I have any questions." She finished the phone call and was hanging up when Shaye sat down.

"You look irritated," Shaye said. She reached for a pink-and-white soft mint in the dish sitting on Elle's desk. "What's up?"

When Elle finished, Shaye rolled the candy around in her mouth, looking thoughtful. "You don't have to do this if you don't want, Elle. I can go instead."

"I think we've already crossed and burned that bridge. He wants me to be the one. I'll be there because that's what we just agreed to."

"I'll come, too. Just in case there's some kind of weird ambush planned."

"That would be stupid for him to do."

"But he's the one who told the press where you were going on your date with Ahmed, so…"

Shaye had a point. Being an idiot was not only reserved for Ahmed Clark. She winced at the thought of the man she'd shared her body and more than a small part of her heart with.

"You don't have to come with me to this meeting. I'm a big girl. I should act like it and handle this thing on my own." Elle sighed and sat back in her chair, the leather hydraulic seat hissing with her movements. She nibbled on the inside of her lip, trying not to worry about what she would confront at the radio station. Then wasn't surprised when Shaye, after kicking off her shoes then looking quickly at her watch, asked her again what happened between her and Ahmed.

After leaving his house late Tuesday evening, she'd gone straight home to shower then sleep. The quick morning meeting with a potential client had gone well, then Elle had her pre–radio show coffee date with Ahmed. She thought.

"Are you going to tell me, Elle?"

God, she felt so stupid. "You probably already guessed, but I slept with him."

"Yeah, I got that from what happened on the radio this morning." Shaye's mouth thinned into a hard line. She left her chair to sit on the corner of the desk and took Elle's hand in hers. "So what the hell happened between the naked riding and you guys being on the radio show? He was savage to you this morning."

Shaye's concern and anger on her behalf made Elle

want to cry. She squeezed her friend's hand. "I honestly don't know. I thought we'd agreed on a certain direction." She remembered his possessive insistence on meeting her the next morning, the way he held her close while they were in his bed. Nothing that happened between them last night should have led to the humiliation of the morning. "I don't know," she said again, her chin beginning to wobble.

No. She wasn't going to cry.

"Well, screw him." Shaye gripped Elle's hands and gave a determined smile. "We'll get you under another man soon enough. He's not *that* damn fine or irreplaceable."

Elle wished she could agree. Every single night since she'd met Ahmed Clark, she had dreamed about him. He was already in her mind and in her heart. A tear splashed down her cheek.

Her best friend looked stricken. "Oh, honey..." She pulled Elle to her feet and into a tight hug. They stood together for a long time, Elle breathing in the comfortable and familiar scent of the one person in the world who loved and accepted her. Who would never hurt her.

"It'll be fine," Elle said, her voice muffled in Shaye's hair. But she didn't really believe it.

When Shaye left for her own office and the next appointment, Elle opened their accounting software to deal with their books. She was elbows deep in numbers, profit and loss—*your business is close to failing*—

when a cheerful knock sounded on her open door. A pretty woman in a crop top and jeans smiled at her.

"Hi there!" The woman looked happy to see Elle, the sleek bob of her hair like its own separate animal, still moving even when the woman stood still. She carried a small white box in her hands.

"I don't have any appointments for the day. You must be looking for Shaye."

"Not at all, you're exactly who I'm looking for." The woman glanced around the office, eyes lingering on each item she saw as if memorizing its details to share later. "May I come in?"

"Um...sure." Elle minimized the accounting program on her screen and waved the woman to sit on the couch. "But I don't understand."

"I'm Aisha," she said, sitting on the couch. And when she didn't get whatever response she was waiting for from Elle, she rolled her eyes. "That brother of mine. Ahmed."

"Oh!" Elle stumbled on her way to sit on the couch beside Aisha then changed her mind and sat on the front of her desk instead, not sure her suddenly unsteady feet would make it to the couch anyway. "What can I do for you?"

"You can't do anything for me, but I hope I can help you."

Elle felt confused. And a little disconcerted. "Sorry?"

"My brother made a big mistake this morning, and he knows it. Because he won't let himself say that to you right now, I came to apologize for him."

Aisha looked uneasy for a moment, toying with the box in her lap. She looked both very young and very tired at the same time. "I heard you and Ahmed on the radio. It was awful."

Heat rushed through Elle's face. Just when she thought things couldn't get any worse. "Oh, my God. Please..." And she felt the humiliating prick of tears. *Not again.* She curled her fingers around the edge of the desk and bit her tongue.

Aisha jumped up from the couch. "I'm so sorry. I didn't mean to make this happen." And she stopped in front of Elle, the white box still in her hands. She shoved it at Elle. "Here! I brought you cake. Ahmed said you'd like it." Then when Elle didn't take the box, she dropped it on the desk near Elle's hip and pulled Elle into her arms. The tears spilled out, hot and fast, down her face and over Aisha's shoulder. She felt Aisha's blouse getting wet under her cheek as Ahmed's sister made soothing circles on her back.

It was a long time before Elle could pull herself together and let go of Ahmed's sister, her face burning and her sinuses well and truly clogged. "Well, this is humiliating." Her voice came out in a croak. She wiped her face with a tissue from her desk.

"That's not what I wanted when I came here." Aisha wiped at her own tears with the back of her hand then muttered a thanks when Elle gave her a tissue. She mopped her face. "I just wanted to fix what my brother broke. You seemed so nice on the radio, and Sam said you and Ahmed had a really nice time on your date." She babbled on. "And you must think he's all right. You liked him enough to have sex with him."

Elle flushed again. "Did Ahmed tell you that?"

"No." A look of mischief crossed Aisha's face, and her smile flickered brilliantly back to life. Her mood swing was giving Elle whiplash. "But I know my brother. Even though he likes to think he's a player and doesn't do emotions, blah, blah, blah—" she made circles in the air with her index finger "—he hasn't been with any women in a while. I think he's gotten tired of the whole runaround. He's ready for something better. For something good." She looked at Elle meaningfully, blinking. "I mean he's ready for you."

"Yeah, I think I got that much from your hint." Elle stood up and turned away from Aisha to pace the short length of her office. Her unexpected visitor brought back all of the earlier agitation and sadness she'd managed to suppress by burying herself in work. "He's not ready for anything more than a lawsuit," she muttered and pressed a hand over the ache in her chest. "After the way he talked about my business, putting it at risk." But strangely enough, Romance Perfected had had a steady influx of clients since the morning's radio show. If things continued the way they were, they'd have to hire an assistant soon.

Aisha opened the box she'd brought. She plucked a red velvet cupcake from inside and, after tilting it toward Elle with a questioning look and getting a quick shake of Elle's head, began nibbling on its edge. She made a soft noise of appreciation and Elle watched her with a glimmer of amusement. Had she brought the box for herself or for Elle?

"He's not the most in touch with his emotions but he's not a bad guy," Aisha said between bites.

"I…" *know*. But Elle didn't say it. Instead she looked away from Aisha and the rabbit-like sounds of her nibbling.

Something of her discomfort must have shown on her face because Aisha stopped chewing and took the pastry from her mouth. "I'm sorry. My mom's always saying how inappropriate I can be." She dropped the cupcake back in the box. "I didn't come to make you feel weird or anything, I just wanted to let you know that Ahmed…he loves hard, and the things he said to you this morning… A girl messed him up a few years ago, so he's always going to be suspicious even when paradise is looking him dead in the face. I know it's an excuse not a reason, but—" Aisha broke off with a sigh.

She put back the pastry box on Elle's desk, brushed off her hands and grabbed her purse from where she'd left it on the couch.

"Just give my brother a chance. It may not seem like he deserves it, but he does." Then she smiled wide, showing off the gap between her straight white teeth. "Plus I've always wanted to have a princess for a sister." She darted in, quick as a hummingbird, and kissed Elle's cheek, leaving a hint of cream and sugar behind.

"See you soon, I hope," Aisha called out as she disappeared down the hall.

Elle stared at the empty doorway of her office not quite sure what had just happened.

If Aisha's goal had been to make sure Elle didn't stop thinking about Ahmed, she succeeded. That night, she dreamed about Ahmed as she'd seen him the night they shared a bed, his body slippery with sweat and hard with muscle as he moved over and inside her. Elle woke up gasping his name. She had a few variations on the dream over the next few days, each more explicit than the last, right up until the morning of her meeting with Clive and DJ Don Juan at the radio station.

To counteract the effect of the dreams, she wore her most severe outfit—a knee-length black dress with a high boat collar and capped sleeves—and she arrived thirty minutes earlier than the time they agreed on. Her one concession to color was a pair of scarlet high heels and matching bag.

But as soon as she walked through the door, Clive called out her name.

"Elle!"

Wearing one of his signature Hawaiian shirts, he walked toward her with his arms held out as if he was about to hug her. She clenched her teeth and kept walking into the building, tempted to look around and check for a camera. How had he known she was coming just then? There had to be cameras. The tap of her heels against the tiles sounded tentative even to her own ears.

"Clive," she called back, hoping her smile was more genuine than it felt. "This is quite a welcome."

"Well, I didn't want to make you feel neglected." His voice boomed down the hallway, and she was grateful when he lowered his hugging hands and only offered a handshake once they were within touching distance of each other.

"You'll never have to worry about that," Elle said. She tucked her red purse over one shoulder and slid her hands into her dress pockets. "Should I head to the studio now or wait until nine thirty?"

"Let's go my office first. As promised, I'm giving a refund for half the money you paid for advertising. The check is on my desk."

"Okay." Elle pursed her lips, unable to hide her doubt. She'd paid for the spot online. There was no need or reason for him to give her a physical check. "After you," she said.

But he insisted on having her go in front of him, and as they made their way down the wide hallway toward his office, he paused to greet nearly everyone they passed. Finally, he opened the door to his office then stood back to allow Elle to walk ahead of him. As soon as she walked into the office, the door closed behind her. A lock turned, and she was trapped in the office with Clive. And Ahmed Clark.

Ahmed jumped to his feet, obviously surprised to see Elle. "This isn't funny, Clive."

"Nobody's laughing, Ahmed."

Elle stood near the door. "Is this where I call my lawyer and start my harassment lawsuit?"

"No. This is where Ahmed apologizes and we can all get on with imagining the ever-after you two will have together." Clive looked between the two of them like they were being stubborn and unreasonable in not giving him what he wanted.

Ahmed stood in front of his hastily vacated chair, a muscle ticking in his jaw. He looked pissed. And not in the least ready to give an apology. Even though the farce—another one starring Ahmed Clark—just started, Elle had had enough. She turned and grabbed the door handle.

"Elle, wait." But it was Clive who spoke, not Ahmed. She shook her head and kept going, wrenching the door open and stalking out into the hallway and toward the front doors. It seemed like everybody was intent on Ahmed's apology except for Ahmed himself, and she wasn't going to wait until hell froze over to get it.

Clive could keep the damn check.

She got back to the office after nearly an hour of driving aimlessly around the city. Her anger had blown away, leaving only exhaustion and sadness behind.

"Elle, is that you?" Shaye called out as soon as she walked into the door.

"Unless someone else stole my body when I wasn't paying attention."

"Come here, girl. Stop messing around. You've got to hear this."

"What are you talking about?"

But Shaye practically came running down the hall, a big smile on her face, to drag Elle into her own office. The radio was playing from her computer, and Ahmed was on the air.

"I do not want to hear that man's voice," Elle said. It hurt too much.

"Just listen!" Shaye turned up the volume.

Not in the mood, Elle heaved a tired sigh and rolled her eyes. But since it would've taken energy to resist Shaye, more energy than she had in that moment, she dropped heavily into Shaye's couch, an old-fashioned granny affair that was much more comfortable than hers, and tried to fix her attitude.

"—I was stupid," came from the radio feed in Ahmed's deep and commanding voice. "And even though I know I made a mistake, and believe me I've made plenty in the past, I've never been more moved to make an apology as I am right now. Elle, I was wrong. I was stupid. Forgive me. Please."

"This is so freakin' romantic," Shaye gushed and sank into the couch beside her.

"What's going on?"

"Ahmed Clark. He's telling you he's sorry."

Elle didn't believe it. "He doesn't mean it. His family and his boss are practically forcing him to say this—"

"They're not."

Elle drew in a shocked breath at the sound of Ahmed's voice, not on the radio but in the doorway of Shaye's office. She jumped to her feet.

"What—" But the mad thud of the pulse in her throat prevented her from saying anything else.

"The show was prerecorded for today." He walked through the door, his steps timid and tentative—words she would've never used before to describe anything he did. Ahmed touched his watch without looking at it.

"But…why?" A prerecorded show was something he said he would never do. Too inauthentic or something.

"Because this is important," he said, gesturing between them. He took a breath that seemed to shake his entire body. "Elle. Gabrielle Marshall. I know this might be too soon, especially after how I acted today, and the last time you saw me and just about every time we've been together, but I'd like—" Ahmed roughly shoved his hands into his pants pockets "—I'd very much like the chance to fully apologize to you and make you understand all of this."

Elle's heart turned over in her chest, a painful shifting that made her gasp and clutch at her middle. "I don't know…" But she was already taking a step toward Ahmed. The twin feelings—wariness and anticipation—twisted her inside out. "You hurt me," she said to him in a voice she hadn't heard from herself since she was a child and trapped in foster care with monsters who hurt and took advantage of her.

"I know. And I'm so sorry for that." Regret thinned Ahmed's mouth. "But please give me a chance to make things right. Here." He tucked a folded piece of paper into her hand. "If you can, come here tonight. I'll explain everything." Then his eyes flicked to look over her shoulder. Elle turned in time to see Shaye give him two thumbs up.

Oh, God...

Elle crumpled the paper in her fist without looking at it. At his flinching look, she only nodded sharply once. He gave her a slower version of that nod then turned and left. In the quiet he left behind, the sound of her own heartbeat was unnaturally loud in her ears.

"So, what are you going to do?" Shaye asked, face serious, even a little concerned.

Elle stared at her best friend in challenge. "Aren't you going to tell me what I need to do?"

"Nope. This is your fight. Your win or your loss. I realize I've been butting in where it's none of my business. I want you to be happy, but I don't want you to think whatever happens from now on is my fault—good or bad. Make your own decision, sweetie, and I'll be here for you whatever it is."

Did an alien take over her best friend's body? Elle stared at her, not knowing what to say.

"I know, I know. You're getting whiplash, right?" Shaye stood up and made a show of brushing off her skirt. "I'm going to leave you alone to think."

"But this is your office."

"It is, isn't it?" Shaye gave an impish grin. "Then I guess I'll go treat myself to an early working lunch." She grabbed her laptop, phone and massive designer handbag. "I'll see you after lunch. Just call if you need me." Then she was gone.

For a very long time, Elle stood in the middle of

the office that did not belong to her. When she finally left, she still didn't know what she was going to do.

Eight o'clock found her at home. The time Ahmed had written on the paper, 7:00 p.m., had come and gone. After work, she'd taken a shower then, after aggressively convincing herself she wasn't going anywhere, put on her pajamas and parked herself in front of the darkened television.

Chances were for people who deserved them. Right?

Elle nibbled at her bottom lip and stared at the television, imagining Ahmed at the restaurant waiting for her while the chance she couldn't give him slowly withered and died with each ticking second of the clock.

The restaurant he'd listed on that note was the one Shaye planned for their first date. La Bohème Sud. The most romantic French restaurant Elle had never been to for dinner, the perfect date she'd never had. She rolled her eyes at her pathetic thoughts.

Sitting there in the dark, she felt the walls of self-protection settle around her more firmly than ever. Yes, she'd told Ahmed she still believed in love despite the things that had happened in her life, but she was only human. At some point, she had to learn to flinch from the fire.

A rattling buzz from the coffee table brought her mind back to the present. Her cell phone vibrating again. Probably Shaye who, despite saying she wasn't interfering anymore, texted every ten minutes to ask

Elle when she was going to the restaurant, if she was there yet, what kind of crow would she stuff down Ahmed's throat before accepting his apology and the happily-ever-after his eyes promised.

It hurt too much to look at the proof of her friend's hopeless and unfounded optimism. Ahmed didn't want a happily-ever-after with her. Sex, yes. Forgiveness, sure. But that was it.

A sharp rapping at her door made her jump. Elle glared at her phone then at the door as if her friend stood right in front of her. Tonight was one of those nights Shaye needed to—

But it wasn't Shaye.

"Can I come in?"

It was an illusion. It had to be. But the more she blinked at the vision in her doorway, the more real it seemed. Ahmed stood there in a suit tailored to fit his broad shoulders and tall frame. The narrow slacks fit well over his muscled thighs and long legs. He looked ready for a business meeting or church.

Elle opened her mouth but only stuttered half words came out.

"I hope that's a yes," Ahmed said with a ghost of a smile even though worry held the corners of his eyes tight.

Suddenly, she was conscious of the relative mess of her living room. The shoes she'd kicked off and left at the side of the couch when she walked in. Shaye's half-finished mug of tea from the evening before. She threw a quick glance behind her.

"Okay. Sure."

Now it was his turn to look behind him. "I brought a few friends with me. I hope that's okay."

Friends?

After getting her quick but confused nod, he stepped back and a slender man walked in ahead of him.

"Good evening, mademoiselle." The stranger greeted Elle with a smile and faintly accented English. "Forgive us the intrusion, but I hope you won't mind if we come in and set up in your beautiful home."

*Set up what?*

Elle startled when Ahmed's warm fingers settled into the crease of her elbow and tugged her back against him. Although his suit was cool, his body burned hot through the luxe material. "Trust me tonight?" His voice rumbled low.

Like a fool, she nodded.

Moments later, in a blur of chairs and flapping cloth and a rattle of cutlery and low voices speaking in French, a small army invaded her home. Elle watched them march past first into her living room then out to the back patio. "What's going on?"

"Unfortunately for me, you didn't make it to dinner tonight, so I brought dinner to you," Ahmed said. He was still standing at her back, his fingers making warm circles on the delicate skin of her inner elbow.

She refused to apologize for standing him up. He had disrupted her day at the office with what amounted to an order to come see him at a restaurant, not taking into account anything she had to do that day. Or her broken heart. Maybe he was used to women bouncing back from his emotional yo-yoing, but she wasn't like that.

But she was also impressed, despite how much she didn't want to be. Not by the fact that he came and had all these people at his beck and call but because he'd come to her not knowing where the night would lead. Elle sighed, flicking a look down his body.

"Let me go change at least."

The reality was she needed to take a breath. Ahmed in her house was too overwhelming. He took up so much space, his smell was all around her, filling her with memories of what they'd done together, reminding her powerfully of the things she'd felt for him, the desire still thrumming through her veins for him despite…everything.

She escaped to her bedroom. Once there, she stood in front of the mirror, a hand over her pounding heart, staring at her openmouthed reflection.

A long while later, she shook herself out of it enough to get dressed.

She decided on an off-the-shoulder blouse and a blue skirt, something of a more modern style than she usually wore. Another random suggestion of Shaye's the last time they'd been out shopping together.

*Be adventurous*, her best friend was always telling her. *Step out of your comfort zone.*

After slipping into high heels, she went to find Ahmed. But the living room was empty. A lush trail of music, saxophone and the gentle stirrings of a keyboard led her out to the back patio.

There, she gasped.

Her backyard had been completely transformed. On the deck, a table for two covered with a lushly gold tablecloth and set with gleaming cutlery sat underneath gently swaying lanterns that looked like they'd been taken straight from one of the bridges in Paris.

A low platform had been set up in the middle of the yard, and a jazz trio was playing there. A short-haired woman made love to a saxophone while another woman, who looked enough like her for them to be twins, flew graceful hands across a keyboard and crooned a song in French into a microphone. A man stood playing a double bass and tapping his feet to the music. All three members of the trio wore tuxedos with red bow ties.

Ahmed had brought La Bohème Sud to Elle's backyard.

As Elle made her slow way into what had been her plain backyard, the scent of mouthwatering French food reached out to pull her even closer.

"Do you like it?"

Ahmed's low voice came from behind her and aroused prickling goose bumps along her bare shoulders. After a brief touch to her elbow, he went to the table and pulled out one of the chairs for her.

Like it? She absolutely loved it, and she told him so.

Even if nothing else came of tonight, she'd never forget this moment. Elle didn't know what to say. This was more incredible than she could have ever wished for, beyond what she thought anyone would ever do for her even with limitless funds at their disposal. From her memory of her visit to the vibrant French restaurant, Ahmed had duplicated the music there—hypnotic jazz—the richly colored table cloths and table settings, and the smell of the food, luxurious and creamy, that she'd gotten from the kitchen on her single visit to check it out as a potential place to partner with Romance Perfected.

Her trembling legs took her to the chair Ahmed held out for her, she sat down and looked over her shoulder at him while she scooted closer to the table. When he settled across from her, she noticed the small vase of flowers in the table's center—red roses and white peonies—that sat low enough for them to see each other.

"Thank you for going along with his," he said. "I know I haven't made it easy."

"I didn't really have a choice, did I?"

He winced. "Am I being that guy again?"

"You mean overbearing? Yes, a little." But she didn't mind it. Not really.

He shifted across from her, his beautiful body just a little awkward. Just that small bit of imperfection made her think, for a moment, that things could be what she wanted between them. But no, she couldn't afford to be a fool again.

"What do you want to eat?" Ahmed picked up a small menu from the edge of the table.

But she couldn't do this. Not yet. As beautiful as it all was, the music and the delicious smells coming from her own kitchen, it was all a little too much. She bit her lip.

"Why are we here, Ahmed?"

He settled his arms at the edge of the table and watched her, sighing. "All right." His hands stretched across the table and around the flowered centerpiece, his palms up and empty. "Will you forgive me, Elle?"

She looked down at his upraised palms that lay across from her, waiting to be filled. She let them rest there, curling her own fingers in her lap to stop herself from simply giving in and holding on.

"I'm ready to tell the whole world what I did wrong," he continued. "By tweet, on the airwaves, in skywriting, if you need me to."

"But what exactly am I supposed to be forgiving?"

"I knew you wouldn't make this easy for me." The corner of his mouth twitched, although Elle couldn't tell if it was from of amusement or nervousness.

"If easy is what you want, then you came to the wrong woman."

"There's no other woman I want." The sincerity in his eyes warmed her like the sun. "I've known this for a while now, but I let certain things from my past mess me up—that woman you saw at the party and all the bull she put me through. I knew better, but my fear got the best of me."

Elle swallowed, remembering clearly the woman in red and her poisonous attitude, the way she'd tried to insinuate herself into Ahmed's life that night. Her own jealousy aside, Elle understood all too well the power of the past and its potential to wreck the future. She'd fought a long battle with her own demons to be the person she was today. Far from perfect, but getting better.

"I know what I just said is pretty cliché, it's nothing new. But, please, can you forgive me for what I did?" A sharp line settled between his brows, worry and pain.

She didn't have to think long about it. "Yes. I can and I do." How could she not? He'd come to her more than once now and with reasons she could understand.

"And there's something else," Ahmed said.

Elle swallowed past the thick anticipation and nervousness in her throat. "Tell me."

"I want to try it with you, seriously try. I know I have trust issues, but I also have an Elle issue." His faded smile appeared again. "I want you in my life, I need you in my life. Please say you'll try to make this work with me."

The tight press of her fingernails into her palms made Elle realize just how tightly she had been clenching her fists in her lap. She wanted to release and lean into what he was offering. But did she even know what he had waiting for her in those open hands of his? She flickered a gaze down to his empty palms then back up to his face.

"Ahmed, I…" But she didn't know how to continue or what else to say. She wanted this thing with him. She could admit that now. But other than another evening in his bed, what did this mean for him?

When she said nothing else, Ahmed closed his hands and slowly drew them back and off the table.

Immediately, Elle wanted to reach out and grab

them. Her stomach twisted around itself in anxiety and nameless want.

"I don't know what you want," she finally said when she could talk again.

Her fingers wound together in her lap, but she refused to look down and cower like a simpering idiot. She looked at a point over Ahmed's shoulder toward the edge of the yard where one of the fence posts needed replacing. Cloth shifted and she felt rather than saw Ahmed move his hands back to the table.

"I want you," he said.

Instead of empty hands this time, a black velvet box lay in the center of one palm. Elle almost jumped out of her seat.

"What…what is that?"

"Exactly what you think it is," he said with the beginnings of the now familiar teasing light in his eyes. "I want you. Will you have me, too?"

Elle's heart began thundering in her chest as she stared down at the box. Ahmed slowly opened it, and she gasped at what lay inside, her hands flying to cover her lips. "You're nothing like my past," Ahmed said, his voice soft and threaded with emotion. "I know that now. That past is over, now I want you as part of my future."

A pink diamond ring gleamed from the center of the velvet box.

Questions tumbled into Elle's mind, one after the other, doubts leaping on top of doubts, but with the opening of the box and, it seemed, of his heart, all those doubts disappeared. There was only one thing for her to say.

"Yes."

"Yes?"

"Yes," Elle said again, and she couldn't stop smiling. Only when she felt his trembling hand around hers did she realize she'd put her hand in his. Their smiles were a matching set.

Ahmed sagged with relief across from her. "Thank God. I thought you'd make me crawl across broken glass to get at that heart of yours."

"You already had it," she said as her smile grew wider. "You've had it since that afternoon in the barn."

He grinned. "Better late than never. I won't bother telling you the day mine fell out of my chest and landed at your feet. Let's just say it was a long time before Valerian."

"I can be a little slow sometimes," she said.

"Never." He stood up and pulled her to her feet while the music rolled and swayed around them. "You're just my speed." Then he dipped his head low to claim her lips with his own.

\* \* \* \* \*

**KIMANI**™
**ROMANCE**

# COMING NEXT MONTH
## Available February 20, 2018

### #561 TO TEMPT A STALLION
*The Stallions* • **by Deborah Fletcher Mello**
Marketing guru Rebecca "Bec" Marks has had eyes for Nathaniel Stallion from day one. Regardless of Nathaniel's naïveté to her crush, her ardor for the newly crowned restaurateur remains intact. And when her romantic plans are threatened, she'll pull out all the stops to prove she's his soul mate...

### #562 HIS SAN DIEGO SWEETHEART
*Millionaire Moguls* • **by Yahrah St. John**
Hotel manager Miranda Jensen needs to marry to inherit her grandfather's fortune. The treasurer of the San Diego Millionaire Moguls chapter, Vaughn Ellicott, offers her the perfect solution. Until she begins to fall for their pretend affair. Will Vaughn choose to turn their make-believe marriage into a passionate reality?

### #563 EXCLUSIVELY YOURS
*Miami Dreams* • **by Nadine Gonzalez**
When Leila Amis meets her new boss, top Miami Realtor Nicolas Adrian, their explosive attraction culminates in a brief fling. Then their affair ends in bitter regrets, leaving Nick heartbroken. A year later, he's back with an irresistible offer. With even more at stake, can Nick make Leila his forever?

### #564 SOMETHING ABOUT YOU
*Coleman House* • **by Bridget Anderson**
Pursuing her PhD while working at her cousin's bed-and-breakfast and organic farm leaves little personal time for Kyla Coleman. Until she meets Miles Parker. There's something about the baseball legend turned food industry entrepreneur that captivates her. When a business opportunity comes between them, can Miles persuade Kyla he's worthy of her trust?

# Get 2 Free Books,
## Plus 2 Free Gifts—
### just for trying the Reader Service!

KIMANI™ ROMANCE

"Ahem." Miranda coughed loudly, bringing her right hand to her mouth.

He glanced up from his conversation, but didn't make any effort to speak. Instead his dark eyes gleamed like glassy volcanic rock as he boldly raked her from the top of her hair to her now aching feet. Pumps were definitely not made for all the walking she'd done today. "Are you done with your appraisal?" Miranda inquired. Flirting could work to her benefit if it garnered his interest. Though he would soon find out she had an agenda.

"Nearly." He continued to scan her critically for several more moments before he beamed his approval and looked her dead in the eye.

"And?"

A perplexed look crossed his features. "And what?"

"Do you like what you see?" Miranda inquired.

"Yes. Yes, I do very much."

Miranda's insides jangled with excitement as she slid onto the bar stool beside him. The bartender came to her immediately. "Have you decided if you'd like another?"

"Actually, I'd like something stronger." She turned to her companion. "What would you recommend?"

He grinned a delicious stomach-curling smile. "Max, get her a bourbon, same as me." He swiveled around to face her. "It's a bit strong, but I think you'll like it."

"I like strong," Miranda countered. "Men, that is."

"Is that a fact?"

She smiled coquettishly. "It is indeed. I noticed you earlier surfing." She inclined her head toward the beach that was about a hundred yards away.

"And did *you* like what you saw?"

She raised a brow. He'd seen her watching him, so she answered honestly. "You know I did. It was quite entertaining watching you out there."

"And afterward?"

An image of him in the wet suit flashed across Miranda's mind. "The view wasn't bad either."

Her stranger laughed heartily and Miranda liked the sound of it. It was deep and masculine and the very air around her seemed electrified being next to him.

"Well, aren't you a breath of fresh air. You actually say what's on your mind."

"Miranda." She extended her hand. "Miranda Jensen."

*Don't miss HIS SAN DIEGO SWEETHEART*
*by Yahrah St. John, available March 2018*
*wherever Harlequin® Kimani Romance™*
*books and ebooks are sold!*

## SPECIAL EXCERPT FROM

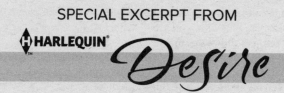

HARLEQUIN®

*Desire*

*Savannah Carlisle infiltrated a Tennessee bourbon empire
for revenge, not to fall for the seductive heir of it all. But
as the potential for scandal builds and one little secret
exposes everything, will it cost her the love of a man she
was raised to hate?*

*Read on for a sneak peek at
SAVANNAH'S SECRETS
by Reese Ryan,
the first book in the **BOURBON BROTHERS** trilogy!*

Blake's attention snapped to the source of the voice.

His temperature climbed instantly when he encountered the woman's sly smile and hazel eyes sparkling in the sunlight.

Her dark, wavy hair was pulled into a low bun. If she'd worn the sensible gray suit to downplay her gorgeous features, it was a spectacular fail.

The woman extended her hand. "Please, call me Savannah."

Blake shook her hand and was struck by the contrast of her soft skin against his. Electricity sparked in his palm. He withdrew his hand and shoved it into his pocket.

"Miss…Savannah, please, have a seat." He indicated the chair opposite his desk.

She complied. One side of her mouth pulled into a slight grin, drawing his attention to her pink lips.

Were they as soft and luscious as they looked? He swallowed hard, fighting back his curiosity as to the flavor of her gloss.

Blake sank into the chair behind his desk, thankful for the solid expanse between them.

HDEXP7140

He was the one with the authority here. So why did it seem that she was assessing him?

*Relax and stay focused.*

He was behaving as if he hadn't seen a stunningly beautiful woman before.

"Tell me about yourself, Savannah."

It was a standard interview opening. But he genuinely wanted to learn everything there was to know about this woman.

Savannah crossed one long, lean leg over the other. Her skirt shifted higher, grazing the top of her knee and exposing more of her golden-brown skin. She was confident and matter-of-fact in talking about her accomplishments as an event planner.

She wasn't the first job candidate to gush about the company history in an attempt to ingratiate herself with him. But something in her eyes indicated deep admiration. Perhaps even reverence for what his family had built.

"You've done your homework, and you know our history." Blake sat back in his leather chair. "But my primary concern is what's still on the horizon. How will you impact the future of King's Finest?"

"Excellent question." Savannah produced a leather portfolio from her large tote. "One I'm prepared to answer. Give me two months and I'll turn the jubilee into a marketing bonanza that'll get distributors and consumers excited about your brand."

An ambitious claim, but an intriguing one.

"You have my attention, Savannah Carlisle." Blake crossed one ankle over his knee. "Wow me."

Want to give in to temptation with steamy tales of irresistible desire?

Check out **Harlequin® Presents®, Harlequin® Desire** and **Harlequin® Kimani™ Romance** books!

**New books available every month!**

**CONNECT WITH US AT:**

Harlequin.com/Community

 Facebook.com/HarlequinBooks

Twitter.com/HarlequinBooks

Instagram.com/HarlequinBooks

Pinterest.com/HarlequinBooks

ReaderService.com

**ROMANCE WHEN
YOU NEED IT**

PGENRE2017

# *LOVE*
# Harlequin
# romance?

Join our Harlequin community to share your thoughts and connect with other romance readers!

Be the first to find out about promotions, news, and exclusive content!

Sign up for the Harlequin e-newsletter and download a free book from any series at

## www.TryHarlequin.com

---

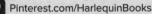

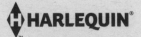